NAYZUN

Enjoy the ride!

by John Biggs

For Milla

and

Rosie Boo

Contents

Part I

Nayzun

In the empty tunnels the Nayzun worked forever. Their hands formed the walls, fixed the rails, kept the strange world alive.

They wanted to be free. They craved freedom. Since one of them had escaped, turned himself into something more than long arms, an eyeless face, long fingers, they knew there was something else out there.

2111, a young Nayzun whose name was simply a prime number, had concocted a plan. And now that plan was coming to fruition.

2111 looked down the tunnel as they worked, fingers plastering stone studded with starlight against the smooth walls. He felt fear for the first time, a feeling he hadn't felt in decades. And he felt hope. The Nayzun whispered to each other of freedom, of where they would go, what they would go back to.

2111 craved freedom.

And soon they all would have it.

CHAPTER ONE

London Rain

The London rain came down in pinprick drops as Turtle Fulton ran across Grosvenor Street. He loved everything about London - the odd black taxis, the double-decker buses, even some of the food. But he hated the way they drove on the wrong side of the road.

He would pause, often, watching for the words "Look Left" painted on the street to remind him he wasn't in New York anymore as oncoming traffic bumped past him. A shiny Mercedes honked at him as he stepped into the rush and he scooted back just before an ambulance, its wee-woo siren blaring and then receding into the distance, roared past. He'd have to wait. After all, the little red man on the crosswalk sign was telling him not to risk jaywalking and he decided to listen.

Turtle kept running in place while he waited, a trick his track coach, Mr. Huff, taught him. Running in big cities was tough but Turtle loved it. Even though all the stops and starts forced him to break his stride every few dozen feet, he loved seeing things from the sidewalk. He loved his plodding pace that let him stop and see the intricate carvings above a pharmacy's front door or the little flowers in a climbing vine on the side of a garage. He loved getting to know a city on foot.

He had run in five different cities in the past five days and he was almost done with the London leg of his journey. It was Friday and the weekend was coming. It was noon in London, which meant it was seven in the morning in

New York. If he hopped on the Mytro in a few minutes, he'd have plenty of time to get back to school.

Mornings were always fun for him now since he began riding the Mytro. He could leave home at six thirty in the morning, take a leisurely stroll to the Mytro stop near his house, and get to school minutes later. Or he could wake up a little earlier, change clothes in a Mytro station, and go for a run in a foreign city. Today he had thirty minutes before he had to be back in school in Manhattan, so he had plenty of time to chew up another kilometer and rush to the Mytro station to get back to school.

He yawned. Turtle had spent a long night tossing and turning. Something was bothering him as he lay in bed the night before and he couldn't quite put his finger on what. The odd feeling had evaporated when he hit the London fog an hour before, but he was still tired. He would have to grab a nap that afternoon after he did his homework and before he visited Agata in Barcelona.

The traffic stopped and he crossed the street.

He ran past a row of brick houses with white ledges and then a bright-green garden behind a high iron fence. Even though summer was on its way, the rain was really coming down now and it was getting colder. Water beaded on his windbreaker and he decided it was getting a little too messy. If he got too soaked, he'd have to change in the locker room and people would become suspicious. After all, it was bright and sunny in New York so, unless he claimed to have run through a sprinkler or a car wash, he probably would have some explaining to do. He decided to take the Oxford Circus stop and cut his losses. Maybe he could come back when it wasn't raining.

Paul "Turtle" Fulton was skinny - he had lost about fifteen pounds in the last year, thanks to his daily runs - and his grandmother called him handsome. He was shy and had black hair and a tight smile, and he lived in Bay Ridge, Brooklyn, down by the Verrazano Bridge. His parents had died when he was very young - he barely remembered them except from photos - but he had his mother's green eyes and his father's dark hair.

His jacket, emblazoned with "Manhattan Friends Track Team," was scarlet and he wore high-tech running shoes that his grandmother bought him and a pair of longer black shorts, not the short-shorts that his track team made him wear. A year before he had been the worst runner on the team and now he was the best, handily beating even Nick and Nate Kincaid in practices and taking out opponents one by one in meets. He had learned a lot in the past year, but he had mostly learned how to run.

His grandmother, however, was already worrying about college essays. He'd have to make up something life-changing to write about and was thinking about writing about his parents. After all, he couldn't very well tell admissions officers about the thing that changed his life - the Mytro - and the girl who showed it to him, a girl named Agata.

It was raining heavily now as he approached Oxford Circus and the pinpricks had turned to big drops. He decided to head home and took out his phone, bringing up an app called 13 as a raindrop plopped onto the screen. After typing in a four-digit security code, he pressed a button marked "Find Me." In an instant, directions to the nearest Mytro stop popped up. First, the map pointed to the tube station entrance and then, with a swipe, showed a dotted line through the station and onto one of the platforms. With another swipe, Turtle saw a series of blurry pictures. The Mytro stop was hidden behind a small door on the main platform. He would have to be quick if he wanted to get into it without anyone seeing him.

The Mytro was a secret train system that ran around the world instantly, and it was the most amazing thing Turtle had ever seen. He first discovered it when his ex-friends Nick and Nate Kincaid showed him a Mytro stop in Central Park, in New York, and he had met his best friend, Agata, when she tumbled through a door a few minutes later. Together, he and Agata stopped a disaster from happening in Barcelona by taking control of the Mytro for a moment, a feat that exhausted them both for almost a month, making them feel as though they had worked out too hard while suffering from the flu.

He and Agata were now quite familiar with the Mytro. They used it to visit each other and to travel the world, and most important, they had a new app that told them exactly where to go and how to find stations. It was so modern that many of the old Mytro riders - riders who met once a month at the Conductor's Guild meetings - refused to use it, depending instead on complex paper maps that had been drawn years before.

When mobile phones became popular, Mytro riders began an exhaustive - and exhausting - process of cataloging all the Mytro stations. Turtle never met these secret riders - the system was huge and only a few people understood or rode the Mytro anymore - but their work was instrumental. It was, in fact, built upon the work done by Agata's father in Barcelona and his assistant who studied at Oxford, Mr. Partridge.

Checking his Casio Pro-Trek watch that showed the time in multiple places - New York, London, Moscow - Turtle saw he had plenty of time. He decided to stop for his favorite bun before he took the Mytro to school.

The bakery was near the train station and was run by an older Middle Eastern couple. Judging by the flag that hung behind the counter, Turtle assumed they were Syrian. They made something they called Chelsea buns, which weren't terribly sweet and tasted of cinnamon and dried fruit. Turtle usually bought one before heading home.

As he turned into the shop, Turtle took a thin paper napkin and wiped his brow. He was still sweating from the run but he was cooling now. The woman - an old lady with a lined face and white hair - smiled at him.

"Good to see you," she said. "Our American customer!"

Turtle smiled. "Good to see you too!" he said as she pulled a Chelsea bun out and handed it over. "We don't have these things back home."

"You should try our Syrian pastry. With cheese. It's very good."

"So I'll take one Chelsea bun and one Syrian pastry then, please," he said.

She smiled and wrapped the second pastry up since he had already taken a big bite of the Chelsea bun. She looked at him and smiled and Turtle blushed.

"Delicious, no?" she asked.

"Yes," he said through his big bite.

After paying from a small stash of British pounds he kept for just such an emergency, Turtle walked out the door. The pastry warmed his hands through the thin wrapper. He put the English pounds into the upper-left pocket of his running jacket. The upper-right pocket held euros. Another inside pocket held Japanese yen and he also had a small stash of US dollars. He had exchanged a lot of his savings - almost two hundred dollars' worth - into various currencies so he could eat and drink weird stuff around the world. He had even tried fried crickets in Seoul, an experiment he would probably not repeat.

At Oxford Circus he stood in front of the station and checked his app. The courtyard in front of the main doors was almost empty. It wasn't quite lunchtime yet and it was past rush hour, but there were still enough smartly dressed passengers to make it dangerous to go digging for Mytro tunnels. Turtle shook the rest of the rain off his jacket and took a bite of his Chelsea bun before tucking the rest in his pocket for later.

He felt a rustle of fabric behind him and turned.

"Turtle, we've been looking for you," said a small man in a trench coat and grey bowler hat. He was soaked and out of breath. "I followed as best I could, but you're a fast one. I hope there's nothing pressing you're attending to?"

8

Next to the man stood a boy about Turtle's age wearing jeans and a windbreaker. He smiled brightly when he saw Turtle.

Turtle beamed.

"Mr. Partridge! Ehioze! Did you follow me?"

"Hello, my friend," said Ehioze. "We followed you a moment, yes. You are very bright!" He pointed to Turtle's bright-red running jacket standing out against the drab raincoats around him.

"When did you get here?" asked Turtle.

"We have been in London for a month. I didn't want to tell you until we were settled. My family lives here now. I brought them out through the Mytro and we are slowly emptying the refugee camp in Italy, person by person instead of all at once so that no one notices when we leave."

"That's amazing. Where are they going?" asked Turtle.

"To different countries to work," said Ehioze. "We tell families we are taking them on a truck and blindfold them. We go through the portable door and bundle them up and go with them to their new home. Then my brother or I take them off and set them right. We have a network now around the world. The Guild are mobilizing to help. Many people are going to France and others are going to the Netherlands and Canada. We've even dropped some in America. We tell them we have access to amazing technology. No one knows what is happening in the camp, but people are excited. We take one or two families a week. It's great fun."

Mr. Partridge cleared his throat.

"Why are you two here?" asked Turtle.

"A bit of a bother, really, and a long story. The Mytratti are reforming," said Mr. Partridge. "And the Conductor's Guild is growing. Ehioze is our newest member. I came to get him, and Agata told me you were in London.

Ms. Banister has called a meeting tonight and we think you should attend. It will be an important one."

He had texted Agata earlier that he would be running in London. They shared their locations regularly, mostly for safety's sake. Agata's uncle had told them they had to watch out for each other and keep the Keys that they both held safe from harm. He texted her when he traveled - even when he went from his home to school - and she did the same. It was nice to have someone looking out for him.

"When is the meeting?" asked Turtle.

"Ms. Banister hasn't said but we will keep you informed. I wanted to come with you, Turtle, back to New York. We can chat on the way?"

"Sure," said Turtle. "I need to go to school, but I can help after,"

"Excellent. I have business to attend to in the morning," said Mr. Partridge. "When you are done with school, we'll come back for the meeting. Let's stay quiet for a bit, though. Loose lips, etc."

"Why?"

Mr. Partridge pursed his lips and pressed one finger against them. *Quiet.*

"Mytratti," he whispered.

Turtle nodded and they rushed towards Oxford Circus station as the sky opened and rain poured buckets.

#

CHAPTER TWO

The Builder

Her room made everyone sleepy. She was attached to rows of machines that let out a strange flowing sound, like a brook babbling in a deep forest, bubbling over rocks and then down a short ledge into a deep pool, a watery sound that buried the room in white noise. Those machines were for her breathing, wet and steady. A beep defined her exhalations while the squiggle of her heart rate ran on a monitor next to her head. A machine exhaled - *beep* - for her then inhaled, the bubbling growing louder for a moment then softly falling. Her nurses sometimes stole into her room to rest there.

She was blonde, thin, and pale, and her arms, which were attached to tubes, rested on top of the sheet. The thin lattice of the Mytro burned in her head and her eyes moved rapidly behind her closed eyelids. She did not move, but in her head she was alive and building. It was her favorite thing to do.

Her name was Ruth. She was the Builder.

How she was chosen to be a Builder she did not know. She had been a normal girl who lived in the waking world. But she got sick when she was younger and something came to her in the night while she slept and changed her, and she began to ride midnight rails through endless tunnels. She stopped in strange, small rooms and watched men and women board old-looking trains. Some of the rooms were in disrepair so she fixed them, rebuilding broken tile walls and smoothing track beds. She swung from station to station in an instant, and in this motion she felt joy for she was moving, doing, making, even if only in her dreams. Some nights she felt like smoke sneaking under a door jamb. Other nights she felt like a monkey jumping from tree to tree.

How she got here she had no idea. But it was better than the coma she had lived in for a short while.

The dreams gave her power, but they also calmed her. Long ago, when she could still move, she loved to find little corners of her grandfather's big old house and to hide there, making herself as small as she could, covering herself with a blanket to make herself tinier. Then, locked up tight like a pill bug, she would imagine herself getting smaller and smaller and smaller as the air took on a strange hum, like the sound of a TV turned on in another room.

Her dreams made her feel at once safe and small. It was a beautiful feeling. Now that she slept all day and all night, she felt warm and small and safe in her own body. She was as small as a pill bug and as big as the world. She could change, she could fly, she could disappear and reappear. She loved her life.

Ten years before, she had fallen asleep and had never woken up. She had been confined to a bed ever since. Her father, a doctor with a gambling problem, had moved her multiple times in those years but she did not feel the movement. She did not speak; she did not eat or drink on her own. She just existed and she dreamt about the trains and their ceaseless travel.

In her dreams, she could move. In life, she could not. So she preferred the dreams.

When she got sick and was unable to wake up, she was angry at everything. She wanted to lash out but she could not move. She was angry at her father for leaving her at hospitals, at her mother for dying, at herself for letting her body rebel in this horrible way. But now there was no anger, only cool motion through the dark. It was better this way, she had learned. She kept her eyes closed and remained calm.

Don't fight. Don't flee. Flow. She had read that once, above a bathroom mirror in her aunt's house, when she was probably ten years old and before the disease took her. While she had been using her imagination to re-create every room she had ever been in - a pastime that had kept her from going mad in the first few years of her confinement – this message floated back up at her and she suddenly saw it.

Don't fight. Don't flee. Flow.

But some nights she would wake and open her eyes, and a nurse would see her and howl something in a language she no longer understood. They would turn on the bright white lights, doctors would rush in, and she'd close her eyes again, afraid. Other nights there would be no one in her room and her eyes would dart to the far corners, looking for the Demon.

When the Demon came, she felt cold. She felt fear. She felt a presence, something that kept her still and sometimes pressed down on her chest. It was then that she closed her eyes again and kept still, preferring to live inside the matrix of green and grey where she existed and not in the world outside her eyelids.

The Demon was another Builder, a maker of the rails. It was jealous of her and of her power. There were only a few Builders in the universe and this backwater planet had one already. It didn't need two. She was proud to be a Builder and she was confused by the Demon. They could share the planet. She wasn't jealous of the Demon's power because she had power of her own.

Some nights she kept her eyes closed and was visited by someone else, not the Demon. She called him the Boy. He was young – at least his spirit was – and he would show her things. The first time the Boy came to her he brought her to an empty train station in some cold part of the world where wind howled down the tunnels and bricks made of ice crumbled at her touch.

Fix it, said the Boy. He did not speak English but she understood him. *You can do it.*

She did not know how to fix it, but the Boy prodded her.

Fix it.

And she did. She would think about what she wanted there, and her thoughts would repair the bricks, lay the tracks, install tile. How she did it she did not know, but somewhere in the dark, her hands moved and she was able to form things out of nothing.

Once the Boy took her to a dark space where she felt like cold stone was closing in on her. She couldn't breathe.

Breathe, said the Boy. *You can do it.*

She did and the space opened and turned into a cube.

Now build.

She thought about what kind of room she'd like. She added wallpaper, a wooden floor. She added a window, but she found that the window opened on blackness so she erased it. She dreamt of a chair and a little table and some nice plates. She dreamt of a tea set, and she sat down with the Boy, who seemed happy with her.

She could never see the Boy, but for some reason, she could sense the space he took up, as if he were smoke or a puff of air. She imagined him being her age when she fell asleep - about eighteen. He was handsome, with dark hair and hazel eyes. She imagined herself one day kissing him, but it would be impossible in her state, she reckoned. She had resigned herself to being trapped in her body, traveling with the Boy through the tunnels, building stations, repairing walls, making things right again. Yes, she was trapped in her body, but her mind could be free.

And so she existed, the Boy visiting her sometimes and sometimes the pressure bearing down on her so much that she felt she would die. She existed like that without fear or anger or regret because she could move anywhere and be anywhere and she had control.

From the outside, the nurses and doctors saw a skinny girl in a hospital gown connected to machines that breathed for her and fed her. A girl who was turned regularly to prevent bedsores and whose arms and legs had turned to sticks. A girl with blonde hair and, if they could see her eyes, blue eyes. A girl named Ruth who once upon a time ran and walked and talked and was a regular girl until something happened and now she was in a hospital forever, trapped but not trapped, building her only joy.

The Demon wasn't coming as much anymore, and neither was the Boy, but something was happening. The trains were burning, and from deep in the crevices that she had not yet visited, she sometimes heard cries of pain on the rails. But she had no idea where to start looking. She kept searching for the sounds, but they died out as she searched.

Suddenly she inhaled. There it was. The sound. The screams. She moved towards them as quickly as she could, her body far behind her in a hospital, her soul free as a wisp.

CHAPTER THREE

Little Bit

The old man thumbed his rosary as he watched a river of trucks and cars pass his front stoop. He was wearing an old hooded hunter's jacket, faded at the seams, the flannel bare and shiny from years of use and reuse, season after season. His face was hidden under a soft plaid hat and he tipped it up to get a better look at the sidewalk in front of his apartment building.

Although it was the beginning of April, he had a hard time staying warm. These days he wore layers of wool clothes well into the summer. It was dark out now, but the air was soft and pleasant, a sign that the buds would soon burst on the trees lining the side streets, and that the crocuses, thin and green now as chives, would pop into bloom in a few days. The moon was nearly full and cast a brightness on the scene that washed out the neon signs and headlights that were vying for control of the sidewalk.

He had a long face, a long nose, bushy eyebrows and no beard. He shaved every morning, a habit he picked up in the navy and never dropped. This morning he had nicked his chin and a small piece of tissue was still stuck there. He rarely looked in the mirror.

The old man was tired. He hoped they would come back soon. He hoped he could leave soon.

He leaned against the iron fence that protected the front door of his building. It was here where the superintendent left the trash that stank all summer, forcing the old man to walk the three blocks up to the park where, until last year, he sat with his little dog and watched the city and the clouds. This winter his dog was too lame to climb down the stairs and he was too tired to walk to the park, so he stayed here, tending to his silent ministry, enveloped too often in the stink of garbage.

Around last Christmas he decided that he would carry his dog to the park when it got warmer and even found a ripped dog carrier in the trash. He sewed it up with grey thread and now it sat empty near his bed, waiting for warmer weather. Until then, he would climb the forty stairs down to the street and keep watch alone, letting his little dog do its business in the massive expanse of the hangar where, overnight, all the droppings disappeared, cleaned by some invisible hand.

He still had plumbing for himself though, some sort of strange solution that seemed to be embedded directly into the lunar-grey floor and walls of his odd apartment. He gave up trying to understand the place years before, after the time he took the drain trap off the sink and dropped a penny down the pipe, hoping it would ping or bounce, indicating a bend in the pipe. It never did.

It was nine o'clock and the bells of Our Lady of Angels were ringing over Sunset Park. He finished his rosary, put it away in a deep pocket, and turned to climb up to his apartment.

Each of the three floors had a separate smell. The first floor, where an old woman lived, stank of trash and cats. The apartment next to her had no scent, but was, until recently, was filled with a family of Mexicans who used to make the stairwell smell like grilled meats - a beautiful smell.

Each week the woman, Mrs. Garcia, gave the old man lunches to eat. He loved the carnitas and tortillas but didn't care for the jalapeños they put on the plate as a garnish. Even Little Bit wouldn't eat them so he threw them away, wrapping them in newspaper so Mrs. Garcia wouldn't be insulted if they saw the food being wasted.

They had moved out on February 1st and a single man moved in, someone who never said hello to anyone and who never cooked. The old man had learned long ago that if new neighbors didn't make an effort to meet anyone, then they weren't worth speaking to. The old man tried to meet everyone in the building, if only to ensure they understood he was a private person and never invited anyone inside his apartment. He wanted them to know that he had spent years alone in that apartment, and he wanted them to sense that he would probably die there.

The old man shivered and continued to climb the stairs.

As he grew older, he noticed he couldn't smell much anymore, so anything good and warm and tasty was alright with him. He relished these smells whenever he could, and the second floor was a treat. Two Chinese families lived there and cooked fish and garlic and used strange sauces that filled the hall with scents like the ones he remembered when his ship took leave in Hong Kong. He lingered there for a moment. They were cooking fish today. It was rich and deep, a smell he could bite and chew. He took a deep breath and climbed another flight.

His floor was the slowest-going. By the time his worn sneakers hit the landing, his little dog, mostly deaf but still able to hear his key in the lock, was up and snuffling at the crack under his door.

His floor smelled like wood polish because young people lived here with a new baby and they cared for their apartment. His apartment smelled like space, or at least what he imagined space smelled like.

His dog, Little Bit, barked.

"Just me, Little Bit," he said through the door. "Just me."

The old man fished his key out of his jacket pocket but dropped it, and it clinked on the floor. He bent slowly to pick it up. His legs felt like lead recently and his back was no better. He hoped that whatever they had planned for him would come soon.

He slowly opened the door and it squeaked as he did so. In front of him was a fake wall, wallpapered in a floral pattern. Against the wall was a small table where he kept a little mail and an old rotary dial phone that wasn't plugged into anything. There was a power outlet in the wall, but it was also unconnected. The only working outlet was near his bed, and it was connected to a surge protector he had bought a few years before, after an old four-way plug nearly caught fire.

The fake wall was about ten feet square and hid just enough from delivery men and busybodies to keep him safe, though he hadn't had a visitor, even a solicitor, in years. Behind the false wall - all around it, really - was the massive hangar.

The light from the hallway barely touched the first dozen feet of the gigantic room. Far off in the distance, faint blue lights hung from the ceiling. The sound of a train, echoing like a memory, burrowed through the quiet distance. Little Bit the dog shivered as the old man lifted her up to his chest.

The hangar smelled metallic. Cold, like iron ore, like the hold of a ship that carried him across the ocean years before, like dust.

Little Bit came up to him, snuffling. He lifted her into his arms and hugged her.

"You're a cold little girl, right? A little coldie Yorkie."

She calmed at his touch.

He slept on a small bed in the big hangar and a separate room - a shack, really - held his bathroom where three pipes came out of the wall, still connected to the mains. Hot and cold ran fine, but the waste pipe was backing up and he couldn't bring the super in to fix it. He had to be careful what he flushed.

He had a little food that he kept on a metal table he stripped and repainted years before. He didn't need a refrigerator because, for some reason, things stayed fresh in the steady seventy degrees of the massive hangar.

Pulling off his jacket, he hung it on a wooden coat rack that had belonged to his grandfather. He sat down on his single chair in front of a wooden table that he bought with his wife a month after their wedding day. A pale-blue light far above him winked on and then turned to a brighter white, bringing the pocked surface of the table - scratches, circles, and scuffs gained over an entire age of life – into sharp focus. The light was helpful. He could sit and read at the table or listen to a battery-powered radio.

He looked at his wooden bed that he made up tight as a drum every morning – "shipshape" as they used to say in the navy. It looked inviting, but he wasn't sleepy.

He had some library books that a boy delivered to him. He picked one up - *Holy Blood, Holy Grail*, a book about mysteries and strange castles. He chucked it back down onto the table.

The dog fell asleep in his lap and he transferred her to the bed. She grumbled in her dreams, her legs kicking slightly as he lay her down on the bedspread. He checked the time. It was late, almost midnight.

He took off his shoes, lay down in bed, and dreamt of a time when he shared this apartment – an apartment of only two rooms filled with plenty of light and parquet floors - with his wife and young child. He woke in tears once in the night and then tumbled back into sleep. The little dog gruffled and huffed in its sleep, its small paws running nowhere against the covers.

He hoped that whatever they had planned for him would come soon.

CHAPTER FOUR

Noises in the Dark

Turtle, Ehioze, and Mr. Partridge faced the station, one of the biggest in the city. It was recently remodeled, and the facade was made up of three bold towers with wide arches between. The station, in fact, looked a little like the Earth Station they had visited a year before in the Breach - something someone with a lot of money or a lot of power would build.

They walked through the front doors, down a gently sloping, grey corridor and came to the ticket gates. Turtle tapped his Oyster card, a card that let him get into the London tube. Mr. Partridge had purchased it for him, and Turtle refilled it with his allowance money. Ehioze, not surprisingly, had his own card. He was already at home in London.

"Mrs. Banister is enrolling me in private school," said Ehioze when Turtle's eyes lit up. "The school gave me a card."

They pressed through the gate and then down onto the platform that the "13" app on his phone had indicated. Turtle looked back at Mr. Partridge, but the little man kept quiet.

To anyone else at the end of the main-line platform, the two tall boys and the short man wouldn't look terribly suspicious. But they had been careful regardless. They waited until the platform cleared off and the last train had rolled away. A few people stood on the opposite side, waiting for the other train, but they were clustered around the stairs at the front of the tunnel.

With a few moments before the next passengers came down to the platform, they went on a small green door that was hidden in a deep alcove and nearly in the shadow of the tube tunnel.

To get through the door they had to unscrew a large hand crank that turned counterclockwise and pulled away a set of bolts. Someone had painted an ornate number 13 on the door and the crank was well-oiled and moved easily, a rarity in this tube station.

Mr. Partridge hissed and pointed up. Security cameras. Turtle knew that London had the highest concentration of security cameras in the world. Even though passengers at the other end of the platform wouldn't be able to see them, the cameras could. Mr. Partridge poked his head around the edge of the alcove and looked up and down the empty track then along the wall. There were no cameras pointing at the alcove, an unusual situation and one probably orchestrated by whoever used this Mytro station.

Turtle looked around to see if anyone on the opposite platform could see them but there was no one there. Mr. Partridge nodded curtly.

"All clear, lad," said Mr. Partridge.

A train in a nearby track pulled in, its brakes hissing and squealing. Under the cover of the train noise, Mr. Partridge and Turtle pulled the panel open. Behind the door was only a blank wall with the number 13 painted on a discolored brick. Turtle checked the app again but there was nothing there, no advice on what to do next.

"Sometimes the old ways are best, Turtle," whispered Mr. Partridge. "The oldsters used to put in an odd brick. It wasn't immediately obvious but..."

"Open sesame," whispered Turtle.

"Open sesame, indeed," said Mr. Partridge.

He pressed the brick with the number on it and the wall opened like a door, the bricks behind the panel moving away from them and swinging into another world. For a moment, they had clear passage to the other side and they rushed in. Ehioze quickly shut the little green door behind them and turned the mechanism from the other side. A moment later the bricks reformed.

Turtle loved this about the Mytro – everything could be normal, you could be at the end of an alley or in a school basement or on a tube platform and then, with a single tap, everything was different and nothing could ever be the same.

The Mytro had changed his life a year before. One minute he was running in the park and then he followed two classmates into some bushes. The next minute he was on a secret train platform under a rock that took him anywhere in the world in the blink of an eye. The adventure - and danger - he experienced that day changed how he looked at the world, and the battle he fought earned him a group of new, amazing friends.

There was Mr. Partridge, the Conductor's Guild secretary, who they had met in Italy a year before. There was Ernesto Llorente, Agata's uncle; and Mrs. Banister, a librarian turned Mytro expert who only rose to power a few months before; and finally, there were Agata and Ehioze. Those were just the Guild members Turtle knew. Mr. Partridge said there were many more - just as there were many more who used the Mytro but did not tell anyone about it. Many of them were in hiding, waiting for the right time to reappear.

With the green door closed behind them, Mr. Partridge finally relaxed.

"Good show," he said. "This is always a tricky station. Now, if I understand it correctly, Ehioze, you have to get to your exam. You take the first train and then Turtle and I will head back to New York."

"That works," said Ehioze. "I'll see you tonight." He hugged Turtle good-bye.

"I'll see you soon," he said. "I'm so happy you're here."

The King's Cross Under station had been built in 1910 (Turtle knew this because of the large stone tablet above the door) and was covered in grey glass tiles. The platform was meticulously clean white marble, and a length of track in front of them led off into darkness in either direction. It looked well used, but Turtle had never thought to try it. After all, they could only enter from one side, not exit, for safety's sake. They were trapped in there once the bricks whooshed closed behind them.

Ehioze boarded the first train that came, a Redbird that looked as new as it looked sixty years ago when it was made in a secret manufacturing plant in New York. A copy of the original Redbirds, these trains showed up sometimes in place of the much older train cars built in the 1800s, cars with wicker chairs and little gas lamps. The Redbirds were mostly powered by electricity - as far as anyone could tell - and rode a bit smoother than the original cars. Ehioze boarded and waved through the window as he rolled into the darkness at the end of the platform.

Mr. Partridge watched him go and then turned to Turtle.

"Ehioze already knows this, as do many of the Guild. There is a problem, Turtle. Since we last spoke, the balance of power has shifted. Mr. Goode is free as is Mr. Kincaid. We don't know what he's up to but we've lost track of him, which is never good. The Mytratti are working on something, something worse than before."

"Like what?" asked Turtle.

"We don't know," said Mr. Partridge, "but I'm headed to New York to find out a bit more. They're manufacturing something big and spending a great deal of money. Some of the original Mytratti are upset at the outlay."

"Then I'll go with you," said Turtle. "I can show you around."

"That won't be necessary, plus, you have school. I have one stop, in a place called Sunset Park, Brooklyn, then a visit to a place called Industry City, and then I'll come and meet you wherever you please," said Mr. Partridge. He handed turtle a slip of paper.

"I've written down the addresses here," he said. "It was standard procedure with Agata's father, to always be able to check in."

Turtle nodded. "So when you're done, come to the Central Park Mid - West stop. I'll be waiting there for you at three o'clock."

"Sounds delightful. Might we have some New York-style pizza?"

"We might," said Turtle, smiling.

They boarded the train to New York and were there a moment later.

CHAPTER FIVE

Steel

The sound of the metal stamper was, for a moment, deafening. A sheet of thin steel had been fed into the machine and a large press came down onto it with a clang, producing a perfect egg shape. Claude pulled the half shell off with a tool he had machined himself and dropped it onto the floor. It sounded like New Year's for a moment, all bangs and clatters, then the press reset itself slowly, and Claude grabbed another metal sheet and fed it into the clamorous machine.

In days long gone, longshoremen loaded and unloaded the great ships of New York in these warehouses that were now home to industry. The first few buildings, the ones closer to the road, were an artisanal hotbed where fancy food makers worked. 13 Steel, Inc. was not one of those.

This was an old-fashioned machine shop – a smaller one, to be sure – but they didn't need much warehouse space and they still dealt in steam and steel and grease. It was a three-man project, and they had been in the warehouse since January, building… something.

Every morning the smell of baking bread would waft through the cracks in the old brickwork and turn the huge main room where three men worked into a sweet shop. Afternoons brought smells of chocolate and ham. The evenings smelled like beer, and laughter trickled through from the outside when a biergarten opened for business in April.

But 13 Steel was always closed, and the three employees never talked to the other people who worked in the Yards. They came and went quietly, locking the big double doors and never going out for lunch.

Claude, an overweight Frenchman who drank whole cartons of milk all day and had studied engineering at Stanford, was speaking with Lionel, a computer programmer with a bright-red Mohawk. The final 13 Steel employee was Pawel, another engineer who knew his way around a welding torch. They were building pods.

None of the three employees were happy with the arrangement, but they were well paid and told that their work was very important. So they stayed quiet, but Lionel was getting bored.

Why were they building pods? No one knew. They had been tasked with building four hundred of them using some of the simplest tools known to man. They had a forming press big enough to stamp out the egg-shaped pod parts, and then Claude and Pawel added the hinge, the locking hasp, and four small legs that kept the pods from tipping over. The pods were six feet long and completely empty, and they had completed thirty of them. Given that Claude had a background in engineering, Pawel had worked on oil rigs, and Lionel had a graduate degree in computer science from Carnegie Mellon, all three employees suspected that their work was a bit below their pay grade.

Every week a truck came to take away the pods. And then they built more.

Lionel had been instructed to model what would happen to the pods at various accelerations. What that meant in theory was a simple stress model on these eggs made of steel. What it meant in practice? Lionel had no idea.

He would send his findings to an anonymous email address and wait for the next request. He even made little models using a 3D printer to test the various shapes of egg they could make - although they had only one mold. Pawel and Claude were content just talking with each other about the news of the day, but Lionel was curious about what he was building.

Each evening he would move his work onto a USB drive and put it into his pocket. He would share it with a group of friends - all programmers like him - and no one could make heads or tails of it. It was like he had been tasked to build a small part of a bigger plan and he could not see the center. That was all well and good when the project made sense, but Lionel thought that making electronic models of huge steel eggs was not a good use of his time.

The pay was good though, he thought, as he ran another model. Claude and Pawel were talking about the woman they had seen making chocolate bars in the factory area next to theirs. They had never tried the chocolate or even talked to the woman, but it was early and they were busy building pods and there was so little else to talk about that they might as well prattle on and on.

Then Lionel got a text message.

Double time. We are preparing to launch.

It was from Mr. Goode, their boss, the guy who paid the bills. He rarely contacted them anymore - he just told them to buy steel and make the pods - but now he was asking for something very specific and very hard. They had made thirty in two months. Now the boss wanted thirty per month. That was one a day. It could be done, but the pods would be shoddy.

I'm worried about quality, texted Lionel. *The simulations show we can't make the shells much thinner.*

Buy more steel. Hire new men. Do what it takes.

Easy for this guy to say, though Lionel. They were in the middle of Brooklyn. It was hard to convince an engineer to come to a weird factory and make steel eggs all day. Clearly this dude didn't care.

"Guys, can we make double the pods? Like one per day?" asked Lionel.

Pawel was drinking coffee and watching the video again. He put down his cup and paused the footage.

"Really?" he asked.

"Really, I guess," said Lionel. He glanced over at the video then turned away, shuddering.

They had hidden a wireless camera inside one of the legs of a pod, and the camera sent video to a server that Pawel set up. It was the strangest video they had ever seen.

Pawel pointed at the screen with a pencil.

"I can't figure it out. They're moving the pod to the tracks then they put it on the tracks and it rides forward into the tunnel. The light's on so you can see everything but there's nothing to see. It's like the camera and dolly are riding into squid ink. Then you see that flash, then the other flashes, and then the camera breaks. I can tell from the transmission. It literally loses components. The lens falls off first then the CCD starts to go. Then it dies. It looks like it's going into some crazy harsh environment. I doubt those pods can survive this. It'll be like trying to re-enter the earth's atmosphere in a wine barrel. It's crazy."

The rest of the team gathered to watch it again. Claude grunted.

"He's paying us double," said Lionel.

"I guess we make more then," said Claude. "I can talk to my friend to see if he wants to work for us."

"Look at that," said Pawel, pointing to the screen again, jabbing it. "It just falls apart."

"We're not paid to ask questions. We're paid to make pods. So let's make pods," said Lionel.

"I'm just saying..." said Pawel.

"Less saying, more pods," said Lionel. "But first, some lunch."

CHAPTER SIX

The Oubliette

It was dark. The walls dripped water.

A strange pressure surrounded him. The air was thick and difficult to breathe sometimes, unless that was just his claustrophobia coming back. During the weeks he had been in the oubliette, the feeling of being penned in had been nearly constant.

It was always an even temperature, about eighteen degrees Celsius, he reckoned. It was quiet and he was as alone as anyone could be, but the water was getting stale and the little food he had was running out. He had lost so much weight, he had tied his belt around his waist. He would have to get out sooner rather than later, but until someone came to get him, he was trapped.

To stay sane, he often sat meditating, breathing in through his nose and out through his mouth, letting his mind wander and open. For a moment he wasn't in the oubliette and then, when his mind snapped back to his situation, he was.

He moved between elation and fear, but mostly he was able to turn both off and just sit quietly, imagining maps he had seen, tracing routes between cities, between towns, between houses. He imagined the route between *La Rambla* and the sea, imagined the route from their apartment to the *Arco de Triunfo* then on to the zoo. He imagined paths he had taken through the zoo with Agata, imagined the stand that sold licorice and the little one that sold warm nuts in the winter. Sometimes he imagined the paper maps, and sometimes the memories came flooding back to him – every detail, every noise, every sunburst that popped up between two buildings as the sun rose over the playa.

They had moved him multiple times before they put him here for safekeeping. The last time they moved him was six months before, at least according to his watch. After that, something had changed, and 411 didn't come to him anymore. They moved him during an emergency, leaving him in the dark for two days, and then the Nayzun brought a huge crate of food - mostly protein bars and beef jerky - and told him that it would be a few weeks before they could come to him again. That was months ago. He felt like he was inside a safety deposit box or perhaps a rat trap, awaiting to be let out. He felt small and helpless and invisible.

He slept intermittently. Sometimes he spoke to himself. He thought himself mad.

"I'm Hernando Llorente. I have a daughter and a wife. I am fine. I'm still alive," he told himself. "I am alive," and he'd fall asleep mumbling, sometimes lying on a thin mattress they had brought him, sometimes sitting against the wall, sometimes leaning back against the crates.

He had horrible dreams. He walked the *Barri Gotic* in Barcelona, stopping in the little grocery below his apartment and buying a jug of water, some bread, some olives, some cava. He took it home to his family, his feet savoring each step like a man savoring a fine meal. He came to his dark wooden door and slipped in the key, but it wouldn't turn. He pounded on the door and pounded and kicked and it would not move. It was as immobile as a wall, not even hollow, just the thud of wood all the way through. Dust came through the cracks between the door and the jamb and started to flow as it turned to sand then water. The door fell over onto him, and he was trapped under its unbearable weight. The water roiled over him, and he would wake in a sweat and reach, hands shaking, for a bottle of water from his dwindling supply.

He had a chemical toilet. It had begun to smell.

Yet some days he'd have a sun-dappled dream – he and his brother and wife and daughter on a boat off the beach, sailing nowhere, everything sweet and clean and good. Those dreams made him wish he would never awaken, that he could stay on that boat with the soft rocking, the slosh of the waves against the wood. Sometimes he'd dream about nights on a pier in the Polish lakelands where he worked for a summer as a lifeguard, a job that he got from an ex-girlfriend whose father owned a restaurant and pool. He'd dream of the endless field of stars echoed in the lake, the curling smoke from a fish fry up the road, the clink of glasses and the roar of music from a wedding party that was hitting its second wind. It was a good dream, one that let him wake with some dignity, without fear.

He decided he was mad. Then he decided he wouldn't be.

He decided he wasn't mad. He decided that talking to himself in this sort of situation was normal.

For a period, he recalled every room of his house. In his imagination, he walked through the front door, looked at the couch, the television as he tried to remember every detail of every room, every magazine on every end table, every book on the shelf. He could now close his eyes and remember details he never knew he had known. The book on world subways was next to the Chinese cookbook, and that was next to a political book written by a retired Spanish president. Next to that were a few journals, a book on quantum physics, and a book of funny cat photographs that belonged to Agata.

Why he remembered any of this, why it was so easy to open his head and bring out this information was beyond understanding. He had heard that the brain remembered everything, and now he knew it to be true.

Amazingly, he could remember the collection of spices in the kitchen.

He knew that the cinnamon jar was empty (unless someone had replaced the cinnamon). He knew that the salt shaker was dirty - someone had gotten a splash of some sort of thick sauce on the side and never cleaned it off. He knew the layout of the refrigerator magnets, even the magnetic poetry set his wife had purchased for him a decade before. *Trees - sway - love - rains - silent - woods.* He could remember all the poems, all the random words. *Train-tracks-go-on-and-on.* The rest was gibberish, but he remembered the position of each word.

Taking his glasses off, he rubbed his eyes. His glasses were dirty, so he rubbed them on his shirt and looked around through the blur. Maybe he'd leave his glasses off for good? Maybe if he couldn't see the place he was in he'd have an easier time accepting it.

Mr. Llorente gave Agata her brown eyes and straight dark hair, but luckily, he didn't give her his bad eyesight.

Without his glasses, he couldn't see much in the gloom but he knew what was before him. The walls of the oubliette were wet, gelatinous. He could push them and his hand would sink through about an inch and then spring back quickly with a wobble. The walls were transparent or translucent, made of some sort of material that looked like water. It smelled like the sea in this oubliette. Sometimes he saw large objects pass in the periphery of the room, but each time he rushed to see what they were, they were too far away.

And so, the days passed, one after the other. For a while he marked the time, trying to remember how many hours it had been since he had been placed here. Now he did not.

The worst thing was that Mr. Llorente could have probably escaped. He knew enough about the Mytro to do something - anything - but the Nayzun had told him that he and his family were danger. He withstood this – this exile – for his wife and daughter. That he could never explain himself to them was the thing that tore at him most.

He could send a message to the Nayzun along the tracks, but if he did that, the Mytro would know where he was. The last time he had done that the room he was in filled with fire and nearly exploded. His glasses had nearly burned on his face. The Nayzun had pulled him out just in time and took him somewhere very far, it seemed, somewhere dark. For the first week or so he kept his nose up against the wall, letting the cool damp soothe the burns. He wished he had his glasses.

"I'm Hernando Llorente. *Soy Hernando Llorente*. I am Hernando Llorente. I have a wife and a daughter and a brother. I am fine. I am alive," he said again.

He did not cry – he had stopped crying months before. Instead, he sat in the door and let the walls of this strange place cry for him. And they did, water dripping and dripping and dripping. Dripping forever in the darkness.

I am alive, he thought. And it was true.

CHAPTER SEVEN

The Bell

A bell rang to scare away the ghosts but a ghost came anyway, the smoke of burning incense wafting through its presence and the air around it whispering its song. Curls of ash fell from sticks of burning punk as the ghost listened for the sound of the rails nearby. They were there, close, perhaps a few doors away. But the ghost had to be careful.

The ghost had once had a body. But once he had been cut from the body, the long, grey body that once toiled in the dark tunnels as a Nameless One – a Nayzun – he was able to move anywhere, take over anyone. Be he was still not free. So he came to be free.

The ghost had gone through the neighborhood, searching, but no one there was open enough to hear him ... until ... until the ghost felt this man's presence, open and trusting, willing to listen to every breeze.

The ghost had chosen a bald man with a kind heart, a man wearing a saffron robe over jeans and holding a bowl of cooked rice. The man paused. He looked around, sniffing the air as if searching for the scent of a flower. He had a young face, smooth and unlined, brown eyes, and clean-shaven cheeks. There was something in the air, a mote. There, then gone. Squinting at the altar, he put down the bowl of rice and placed his hands at his sides.

"Who is here?" asked the man.

Although the man could not see the ghost, he could feel him. The ghost knew that the man could sense him, so it weighed its options. Here, in this sacred space, the ghost was safe, but the ghost had to leave soon. It had a job to do. Who was this man in saffron robes? Could he be trusted? The hardest thing for the ghost to do was interact with the world, but this man, a man who could sense him, could be a valuable ally.

The ghost had been wandering the sidewalks for hours when it found this small storefront. The ghost could sense the peace inside the place, so it moved through the front door and looked around, amazed at what strange custom had caused the temple to be decorated red and gold with little golden statues here and there and a plate of oranges and a bowl of rice lying out for all to eat. Then the ghost recalled hearing of the Chinese and their beliefs. Perhaps that was what this was.

I am here, said the ghost.

The man in the robes looked around, his heart racing.

"Where are you?" asked the bald man, the monk.

Near you, said the ghost. *But my position does not matter.*

The bald man heard the voice in his head, in his own language. The voice was a thousand clanging wheels. It was the whistle of the wind through the dark. It was the clang of metal on metal, cacophonous and rhythmic. It echoed in his head. He was frightened.

The ghost could leave and allow the bald man to think it had been all a dream. But the ghost needed help. The ghost was silent.

"Are you troubled?" asked the bald man. "My name is Mark. I am a monk. I am here to help."

What is this place?

"A sacred space. You are safe here."

I am safe nowhere. I need your help. You are the only one here who can feel me.

The bald man, Mark Wu, was a *bhikkhu*. He was twenty-five and had lived most of his life in Beijing, born to American-Chinese parents, both university teachers, who then moved back to Brooklyn. Now he lived in Sunset Park on a high ridge that overlooked Manhattan, and he ran this small storefront temple. The temple was new and there weren't many visitors. It was frustrating, these days, sitting in a quiet room, waiting for supplicants.

Now he had a very strange visitor.

"Do you need to pass to the other side?" asked Mark. It was the first time he had spoken to a ghost and he didn't know what to say.

I need to find an apartment, said the ghost.

Mark looked around as the incense smoke swirled. A bowl of oranges sat uneaten in front of a golden buddha. His ghost needed real-estate advice?

"You want to live somewhere?"

There is a man in grave danger. There are people who will hurt many. We must help, said the ghost.

"Are you a demon?"

No, but I can lead you to one, said the ghost.

Mark went cold. "What do you need me to do?" he asked, as if this was the most normal thing in the world.

He was surprised he was so calm, but for some reason all of this felt right and solid and real. Why wouldn't a ghost come to a place of worship, a storefront Buddhist temple in Brooklyn's Chinatown? Why wouldn't the ghost speak to him, whispering in the incense smoke in a voice that sounded like clattering steel wheels on endless rails? He had waited all his life for this moment. Mark would not let this moment pass.

I will ride you. You will feel me. It will be cold, said the ghost.

"And then?"

We will go to help who we must help.

"Let me change first."

You have little time. Go.

Mark went to the back of the temple and changed into a T-shirt. It was warm outside, but he thought about what the ghost said. Cold. He put on his light leather jacket.

Mark came back out into the main room. The ghost was still there.

"I'm ready."

Suddenly he felt a stabbing cold, a cold that was so surprising that he gasped. He had oce worked at his uncle's grocery for a summer, in the freezer, and this was worse than that, a cold that froze instantly and to the core. The cold was pain.

For a moment Mark saw the ghost's face in the afterimages that burned across his eyes. A young face, a mustache, a soft cap, breeches, brown vest, a length of rope unravelling. Then Mark saw the ghost's other face, long and blank and dour, grey skin pearlescent as the inside of an oyster. And then the cold settled on him like a disease and stayed there.

I am with you, said the ghost.

And, with a shiver, Mark knew that it was true.

CHAPTER EIGHT

BCN

Agata Llorente woke with a start. She had been sleeping as well as could be expected, given her father's disappearance, and she had recently stopped going into her mother's room at night. As she woke, she had felt something strange, something like a voice and something like a presence. It made her heart race and her teeth clench, and she was cold because she had kicked her comforter onto the floor.

At least she wasn't in a panic.

It had taken all her willpower to stop the panic attacks but she finally did it. She would count in primes, just like her friend Turtle did when he ran, and when she got to the bigger numbers, the ones she couldn't quite remember but had to figure out in her head, she noticed that the fear would dissipate as she focused on the numbers.

In the months that followed her first ride on the Mytro, she felt that she was getting closer to her father. A researcher and one of the original Mytratti, her father had disappeared into the Mytro, sending her and her mother into a tailspin. She felt close to finding him, though, and the Conductor's Guild was helping.

In between prime numbers, she'd repeat her mantra. 3...*She would find her father. She would. She would.* 5...13.

Her room this morning was bright and full of sunlight. A copy of her private Mytro map was tacked to the wall and there were pins in it where she suspected – based on her father's notes – that secret Mytro stations, oubliettes, existed. She had just completed a survey of Norway and Sweden with Turtle and had pinned thirty places where the Mytro could hide an oubliette.

When they checked those places, though, they found nothing but dust and broken tile. These were out-of-the-way places built by strange people, designed to trap travelers as they moved through the Mytro. Only with their Keys could they get out, and when they found an old oubliette, they closed it permanently as they left, the space popping out of existence just as they boarded the train and roared down the tracks. It had been scary work and frustrating simply because each oubliette she found had been empty.

She stretched in bed, her legs sliding under the cool sheets, and brushed her long brown hair away from her face. She yawned and finally got out, sliding her feet into a pair of warm slippers for her trip to the bathroom.

Once she had showered, she dressed in jeans and a white blouse and went down the hall into the kitchen. It was almost time for school, but she didn't have to rush because there was a Mytro stop in her attic.

She ate a piece of toast with olive oil and a little smoked fish her mother had put out on the table - she and Turtle had started liking smoked fish after their Baltic adventures - and she drank some tea.

Her mother was somewhere else in the apartment, probably in her own room. In the months since her father's disappearance, her mother had taken to cooking. She was selling vegan hot dogs at the market near their house, preparing the homemade condiments at a small kitchen around the corner and transporting them to a kiosk she rented.

Her father still received checks from his "work" – donations, really, from the Conductor's Guild - so that kept the family going. Sometimes her mother went to London to meet with the Guild. She had gone first to thank the members for taking care of them while her father was away, but now she went to share intelligence. Her mother didn't like Agata to go very far on the Mytro, though, at least when school started. Luckily, some of the Guild members would come and visit her.

Turtle visited weekly, and they would get coffee and churros at the place down the street if they didn't have a mapping mission. Mr. Partridge visited most weekends. Their new friend Ehioze even came by once with his mother, and they made paella together, Agata's mother showing them how to eat the crispy rice at the bottom of the dish called *soccorat*.

Her mother was American and so was always positive, a trait that sometimes infuriated Agata. She had her father's brooding temperament, and she didn't like her mother's optimism, although that often was the only thing holding them both together. There had been storm clouds in her head for months before she learned to take her mind off her fear and anger and to treat everything she did like a complex puzzle.

"I don't want you running around today," said her mother as she walked in wearing her work clothes. She tried to dress very Western with a rodeo shirt - pearl buttons on gingham, lots of fancy pockets - and dark jeans. "Go to school and come home. I'm having a bad feeling about today."

"You too?" Agata asked in Spanish.

"*Sí,*" said her mother. "*Pero no está claro qué.*"

Her mother looked at her intently, then reached out and touched her cheek.

"Like something is happening," said Agata.

"So maybe that's a good sign. Maybe they're close," said her mother. "Try not to worry about it. If we both feel it, then that means your father will be back upstairs puttering round and snoring on Sunday mornings in no time. It's an omen."

An omen. Did Agata believe in omens? It was hard not to, now, given all they had learned. Agata always prided herself on being rational, thinking through problems and working around fear. But as she learned more and more about the Mytro, she discovered that those tactics just didn't work. Now she understood what people meant by "blind faith."

Going into the Mytro was always a gamble. What would happen? Where would she end up? And if she felt the least bit scared, her best bet was to simply leave, to enter another station somewhere else, somewhere more familiar, and move from there. Hunches and intuition were a big part of all of this. A hunch had sent her to New York, and she had befriended Turtle on a hunch. Now her hunch that her father was someplace cold and surrounded by water was becoming clearer. But where?

Her mother noticed her mood darken, so she smiled and brushed a strand of hair out of her daughter's face.

"Do me a favor and get out of your head, Agata. Talk to some of the kids at school. You could use some friends who are local and who don't travel around the world so much," said her mother, half joking.

Agata went to the bathroom to brush her teeth. When she came back, she found her mother preparing mustard at the counter.

"Stay close to Mytro stops," said her mother. "And if someone comes after you, run. We'll get your father back, sweetie. We will."

"*Si, mama,*" said Agata. She kissed her mother good-bye and pulled on her backpack. It took her only a few minutes to get to school now, thanks to the door in her attic. She took winding stairs two at a time and entered her father's study, which she and her mother had cleaned up after it had be ransacked a few months before. She even bought her father a new mouse for his computer, a black and silver wireless model. She wanted to be there when he turned it on for the first time, to see what he thought. She wanted to be there when he came back, period. It was going to be amazing.

The portable door was there, leaning up against the attic wall, still scorched but in slightly better shape than when they had dragged it back from the Earth Station. Long strips of adhesive still clung to the door and it was shattered on the top-right corner. There was a thin patina of ash on it where something hot had smoked and burned it. Turtle had dragged the door down the stairs months before, out into the street, and then dragged it back from the Nayzun's hangar a few days later. It had seen quite a beating.

This time, before she boarded, she decided to take something from her father's desk. It had been sitting there for months, discovered after they had finally cleaned up the mess left by the thieves who had ransacked their apartment looking for the Keys. It was a small silver train car, made to look like the Mytro cars that usually ran on the tracks. It was surprisingly heavy, and Agata suspected that it had been made for her father by one of the Mytratti. Someone had etched a small number 13 in the bottom, the sign of the Mytro. She put it in her jeans pocket, and the weight of it comforted her.

She pulled out her cell phone to read the news before she left for school while she still had Wi-Fi. The email - one note from Turtle telling her that he was in London and a picture of a Mytro station in Brussels from her uncle - was sparse but her newsfeed was full of odd and interesting happenings, especially things related to refugees and migrations. Halfway down one newspaper site was a brief story about mysterious disappearances from a refugee camp in Italy. Agata smiled a little. Then there was a related story. She clicked on it.

Hundreds of men and women were missing in Russia. The police had no leads, but they suspected that a ring had sprung up that specialized in kidnapping.

She read a bit more. Interpol was reporting that the same thing was happening in Paris, London, and in Warsaw. "The net is wide," said a French detective on the case.

Was it the Mytratti again or something else? Agata had learned to see their hand in almost everything, and most of the time she was right.

She wanted to speak to 411, the first Nayzun she had ever met and who promised to help her find her father. But 411 was impossible to find. He had been subsumed, somehow, his body taken away, and his spirit or soul or whatever was left had disappeared down the tunnels. It was a strange experience and one that had changed a lot about how she saw the world. Before the Mytro there was no magic, only loss and distance. After the Mytro there was hope.

Agata pressed her messaging app and sent Turtle a quick hello. No response. Maybe he was still traveling.

She looked at the photos on her father's wall - her uncle and her father, smiling; photos of train stations from around the world; hand-drawn maps of Mytro stations hidden under restaurants and in churches. To the average visitor, the attic would look like the den of an eccentric with a train fascination. To someone who knew the Mytro, it was a treasure trove of knowledge.

She opened the door and braced herself for the slightly topsy-turvy feeling of entering a slanted room. Inside was a small station covered in dark tile with a platform at the end. A Mytro train roared through and stopped just as she opened the door, and she walked through feeling the world right itself slightly as her foot hit the tile floor. The train dinged and she boarded.

"Barcelona English Academy, south basement," she whispered into the quiet train car and then she sat down. The train rushed forward into the dark, and for a brief moment she imagined her father, somewhere out on the rails, working to find his way home.

She would find her father. She would. She would.

CHAPTER NINE

The Conductor's Guild

Turtle and Mr. Partridge got off at a Mytro station hidden in the basement of Manhattan Friends School. A secret group called the Mytratti built the station and the school in the late 1800s when no one quite understood the power and the reach of the Mytro. Instead of simply studying it, the Mytratti built stations, hiring masons and bricklayers to simply shore up the walls in the strange, empty caves where the Mytro ran. Because the Mytro was so strange, they tried to wrap the strangeness in a veneer of train travel. Before trains, however, the Mytratti sent wagons down into the dark tunnels that connected distant places around the world. And before that was a fateful accident when one of the original Mytratti, the youngest of two brothers, tumbled into the dark and disappeared.

The Mytratti had changed in the last twenty years, moving from a group of thinkers and intellectuals and into a militant group dedicated to controlling the Mytro at all costs. The group was even more secretive than the Conductor's Guild. Ultimately, they wanted the Mytro to themselves and only themselves.

Now new stations were popping up in a new style, and something about these new stations was disconcerting, as if someone was taking over the system and remaking it. The old stations were covered with old and beautiful tiles. The new ones were less organic. The Central Park West stop, the first one Turtle had visited a year ago, was now made of cold shining steel and green ceramic. A stop in Manhattan's Chinatown was made of red glass, although Agata thought it was pure ruby.

It could have repair, the way they refurbished subway stations in New York, but even the Conductor's Guild knew little of the perpetrator - or perpetrators. In any case, the Mytro was getting strange.

The station itself was very simple with just a hand-painted sign – "MNH FRIENDS" – hanging on a rusted hook. The tracks, which led off into darkness in either direction, were shiny but old, the spikes used to lay them pitted and red. The door out to the boiler room was made of wood and looked like it had been scavenged from another building. On its other side was a set of bricks that slid away easily when the door was opened.

As Mr. Partridge and Turtle walked out into the boiler room, the steam fogged the man's glasses and he took them off to rub them on a handkerchief.

"I've been told to visit a man in Sunset Park, Brooklyn. Is that far?"

"No, but I'd recommend the subway. I haven't found many stops in that area yet, at least nothing that anyone has written down."

"Ah, doing a bit of mytrunking, eh?" asked Mr. Partridge. "Mytro spelunking?"

Mytrunking is exactly what Turtle had been doing. He spent a few evenings each month riding the Mytro from station to station and would often try odd combinations - 75th Street and 5th Avenue in Brooklyn, for example – just to see where he would end up. He wrote down the stations he found - they were usually about four blocks from each other in a straight line - but there were some places in New York where there were no stations at all. He found that there were no stations in Green-Wood Cemetery in Brooklyn, a rolling, beautiful graveyard that was once a popular picnic destination, nor were there any around Times Square, the heart of New York. There were many that mirrored the actual subway stops, but most of the avenues that went north to south had Mytro stops every few blocks. Turtle kept a journal of the stops he found and reported them in the 13 app.

In addition to the ten public members of the Guild, there were hundreds of others who kept completely silent. After all, people still used the Mytro daily, although they were very quiet about it. In fact, as Turtle quickly learned, there were many people he knew who took the Mytro to and from work and school, not to mention around the world. The owner of the grocery around the corner from him knew about the Mytro and used it to ship produce from his cousin's farm outside Atlanta, Georgia, and milk from a dairy farm in New Jersey. Sadly, the grocery owner couldn't advertise that his fruits and vegetables were completely farm fresh because he would have to give away their source.

Mr. Partridge pulled out a slip of paper with an address on it, and Turtle checked his phone - first the 13 app and then the mapping app. The Mytro charts showed no stops in that area, but the New York subways stopped a few blocks away. Turtle showed Mr. Partridge which trains to take.

"I will meet you this afternoon, after school," said Mr. Partridge. "I'll come to your area, where you grandmother lives. Perhaps we can meet in the sandwich shop around the corner?"

"Mike's Deli?" asked Turtle. Mike's was a dirty bodega near his home run by a pleasant, if quiet, guy whose real name was Amir.

"Oh, yes. I did enjoy the honey turkey he had on offer there. Do you think he'll have more of it?"

"I'm sure they will," said Turtle. "Now we have to get you out of here."

The boiler room opened onto the boy's locker room, which was empty. Mr. Huff's office, around the corner, was dark. They had arrived surprisingly early, Turtle noticed, so perhaps school wasn't even open yet. He'd have to hide out somewhere until the bell rang.

"Why are you going to Sunset Park?" asked Turtle.

"It seems that's where much of the recent Mytratti activity was situated. We don't know what sort or who we'll meet there. We just know that something is going on," said Mr. Partridge.

"Another Breach?" asked Turtle. Less than a year before, a Breach - a station that was about to pop into actual being - was threatening Barcelona. He and Agata stopped it - just in time.

"It seems that way. Someone is sending money through the Mytro now, in cash. A few of our trusted riders followed the bales of dollars out to Brooklyn. It was picked up by a group of men wearing black masks. Then they took something back with them, something big."

"Why?"

"We don't know much at all at this point. It's a bit of reconnaissance. We have a map to the Breach but we can't go there. It's not a station, per se, and simply saying the location won't take us there. It could be something entirely new, or it could be a mistake in the records. That said, we want to know where the money is going and what the Mytratti are up to. I'm not much of a detective, but I suppose I'll have to do."

"I can come with you," said Turtle.

"You have school. We'll rendezvous in the afternoon," said Mr. Partridge.

"I'll text you when I'm out of class and come to lead you to the turkey," said Turtle.

"An excellent plan. Excellent indeed," said Mr. Partridge, smiling. He boarded the train, heading farther into New York, and Turtle quietly left the station, making it to homeroom well before the first bell.

CHAPTER TEN

Spooky Action at a Distance

S eated in the front row of trigonometry class, Agata felt something rustle at the back of her brain. It was a strange feeling, as if someone were saying her name in another room. Agitated, she looked up and out the window at the bright courtyard and the sliver of blue just visible past the top floor. Her math teacher, Ms. Gomez, tut-tutted with her tongue and Agata turned back to face her exam paper. What was it? What was she hearing? She pushed it out of her mind, but it bobbed back in like a leaf floating on a stream.

Thanks to Turtle's tutoring, she was finally doing well in school. Turtle came over most weekends for a few hours, and her mother made them Iberian delicacies - tapas (Turtle loved *patatas bravas*, spicy potatoes with garlic sauce), *jamon*, and, most important, paella. Turtle admitted that, at this point, between his grandmother's paella and Agata's, he was getting a little tired of it, but he ate it anyway, marveling at the long, weird shrimp her mother dropped into the dish as it cooked.

Having read books about massive farms, Agata was now vegetarian. She decided she didn't want to kill any more cows - or long, weird shrimp. It was getting tough around the house, but her mother was patient and a good cook and Agata was learning how to cook lentils and make hummus. Turtle's grandmother was also helping, making delicious vegetarian meals whenever she visited.

"More meat for me," said Turtle, but even he was eating fewer burgers and hot dogs. It was almost normal at Agata's home now, with Turtle visiting, but her father was still gone and that left a void like a broken tooth.

This test was taking her a little longer than she expected. The sines and cosines weren't confusing anymore, but she knew she had to take a little extra time to make sure everything made sense in her head and on paper. She felt really good about the test though. She'd probably get at least a 95 percent because she was unsure of a few things, but she hoped she'd get a perfect score, which would keep her on the honor roll.

Then it was there again, the little voice. The little rustle. She sat perfectly still, trying to catch it.

A brush of cold blew past her neck, raising the hairs on her arms.

Agata. A voice. Her father's voice. It was plain as day. He was talking to her. *Agata.*

Ever since he had disappeared, she had longed to hear his voice. He had never recorded anything, no videos that she could find on her phone or voicemail messages. He was a quiet man, always thinking, and now she was upset that he had gone without giving her even a crumb of his voice. But there it was: her name, whispered in the chill.

She waited to hear it again, but it did not come. She finished the last problems quickly, probably getting them wrong. Maybe this was a sign, some kind of news. Maybe he was home.

She turned in her paper just as the bell rang for the next period. She was usually careful, double-checking everything just as Turtle had shown her, but today was different. She had to get moving. She was happy, but something was troubling her.

She was always troubled now. Her teachers knew her father was gone, but they thought he was working in some remote place surveying plant life. Her father was a scientist, so she and her mother had created a cover story for him, explaining he was now stuck in the South American rain forest indefinitely. Agata even did a science project on his "work," looking up information online about real botanists. No one suspected anything.

Having turned in her test, she left the classroom. In the hall, students were filing out and approaching their cubicles where they kept their books and coats. It was getting close to the end of the day, and some of them were getting ready for advanced study or their internships.

Agata's school was based on a unique model where every senior had to do actual work, whether it was in a restaurant like her friend Maya Grace or in a legal office like Maya's twin brother, Luis. Maya wanted to be a chef and Luis wanted to be a lawyer. Agata hoped to work for a cartographer, a mapmaker, when it was her time to take an internship. She wanted to learn everything she could about maps. After all, Agata's current career goal was to get her father back through the twisted labyrinth of the Mytro.

She walked to her cubby where Maya was already pulling out books for their next class, English. Maya Grace, who had been born in America but now lived in Spain, was about Agata's height, but she was blonde and wore glasses. Today she wore her hair in pigtails and a poppy pin on her burgundy jumper. Years before, the school had required a uniform; now it was a free-for-all. One of the older boys often came into school wearing a bathrobe or coveralls. It was part of the school's "creative atmosphere," and Turtle, who had to wear a uniform every day, thought it was goofy.

Maya smiled at Agata. "How was the test?" she asked.

"Awful, but I think I did OK. A lot of the problems were in the homework," said Agata. "What's going on this weekend?"

"Not sure. What do you want to do?" asked Maya. "Is your *amor* in town?"

They all thought she and Turtle were boyfriend/girlfriend but it wasn't like that. They were friends. She helped him with his Spanish homework and he with her math. They watched movies. They ate tapas ... but wasn't that what boyfriends and girlfriends did?

"I will repeat this again: *el no es mi amor*. But he might be here. Why? Do *you* want to go out with him?" asked Agata.

Maya smiled quietly. Agata had explained that they weren't together and Maya seemed definitely interested. The hardest part was explaining where Turtle went to school and why he didn't speak Spanish, but after a few quiet dismissals, her school friends stopped asking. And, thanks to Turtle's shyness, he never noticed Maya.

"It might be nice to see you two," said Maya coyly. "Where does he live? Maybe we can go there?"

"It's pretty far from Barcelona," said Agata. "He takes the train."

Agata's phone buzzed in her jacket pocket. She reached down to silence it – cell phones were not allowed on school grounds - but it buzzed again.

Pulling it out of her pocket, she activated it and moved to the text messages, scrolling through the those she had received while taking the test. She tapped it and began to read, then looked back up at her friend, and then back down again, quickly.

"What happened?" asked Maya.

"I got a message," she said.

"From who?" asked Maya. "I mean whom?"

Agata looked at the number, trying to make sense of it. 13 13 13. The number sat there, taunting her. Three primes. 13 for the Mytro.

I know where your father is. Where can we meet at the Lucifer statue in Madrid?

It was signed "Kincaid."

Maya looked over her shoulder, so Agata quickly locked her phone and looked up at her friend. She had tears in her eyes.

"I have to go, right now. I'm in history next period. Can you please tell Mister Milagro that I had a medical thing? Something medical?"

"I'll tell him but I'm coming with you. I have internship today and the restaurant doesn't need me. Where are we going?"

"I don't know," said Agata. And she really didn't.

CHAPTER ELEVEN

Burning

The Nayzuns' cries tore at the quiet of the hangar. Fire, red and rolling, and smoke as black as pitch roared through the open space and licked the high places where the Nayzuns slept. The Mytro had been cruel of late, leaving them alone to work for days at a time – weeks, sometimes – and then, on a whim, burning through their world like a storm of red lightning. This time four were burnt, pulled down from the ceiling by the heat. They expired quietly, no noise or movement ... pieces of paper touched to a match, the ash curling silently into a tube of darkness and smoke. One burst of flame burnt them, and the next blew them away into a whirl of dust.

This burning did not free them. It was a permanent death, not freedom. The younger Nayzun, 2111, knew that one of the oldest Nayzun, 411, escaped through some strange quirk of the rails, but the burnt ones weren't so lucky. They would not come back and they could no longer live. They were destroyed. It was the Mytro's ultimate punishment, and it was as cruel as anything 2111 had ever seen, ever imagined. Why it punished only certain Nayzun - or why it chose them randomly - was anyone's guess. It had stopped talking of late and simply rampaged through the dark hangar, mercurial and mute.

Perhaps the Mytro was jealous. There was the other one, the girl. She had come often, surveying the madness and sometimes crying. She seemed to see the Nayzun as they really were, before the change. She told 2111 to take the human man and hide him in a special place she had designed until the Mytro could be defeated. She told him the human man knew the secret to letting the Nayzun go free, so he was absolutely necessary. And so 2111 defied the Mytro for the first time, the defiance feeling strange in his long, stalk-like body, like an acid introduced that would slowly dissolve him.

This, thought 2111, *is what fear feels like.*

Then, when the burning was done, new Nayzuns would come out of the darkness, young ones with less history, ones with a blankness about them that frightened 2111. He had been safe so far. He had avoided the burnings for a while, hiding in the far corner of the hangar when the fire came, but one day he would not be so lucky.

The ones who weren't in the hangar sometimes were spared. Many of the old ones, the ones with numbers under 997, bore the brunt of the abuse. They had helped 2111 hide the humans, and they had colluded with the humans in ways the Mytro never thought possible. Was the Mytro's power slipping, or had it had no power over them at all? That wasn't a question 2111 wanted to answer directly. But perhaps, through the scientific method, they could eventually figure it out. Until then, there was the burning, and 2111 marveled at the violence. Why would the Mytro be so cruel? Why was it so angry? Or was it angry at all?

411. The Mytro was angry that 411 had escaped and it was worried that more would escape. It needed offerings, and the humans were godless now and did not offer up new humans to populate the tunnels. Instead, the Mytro had to call ghosts from faraway places, from worlds that did not have the docility of humans or their kindness, places where the Nayzuns, the Nameless Ones, had lost their names to the howling of the tunnels.

The Mytro made examples of them. It hated the ones who had come from Earth, against their will. They still had old memories, the way a butterfly learns the things that poisoned it as a young caterpillar even though, inside the cocoon, the caterpillar is completely eaten and reborn. That is what the Mytro did. It was the chrysalis of evolution, the eater and the womb. And its children were now willful.

But 2111 knew that new Nayzun were coming from somewhere else, somewhere not distant or strange. They were coming from Earth. Perhaps this would keep the Mytro at bay?

2111 loved humans. He loved how they moved, like skittish animals, and he loved their strange scents. He loved their colored eyes and strange, long hair. He loved their clothing, how embarrassed they were without it, and how far their short, pink bodies were from his long, sinewy arms, legs, and torso. He loved their mouths, the way they stuffed strange foods into them and how they yawned when sleepy. What he wouldn't give to see another human.

2111 could still remember what he was, once, long ago. His kind remembered their lives before the Mytro while none of the other Nayzun could. He had been a hunter on his planet, clad in skins, strong as a storm. His face was long and lupine, his teeth made to catch and tear meat. His arms and legs were covered in hair, and he could walk upright or on all fours, depending on how fast he wanted to move. It had been a wonderful life.

One night, though, he wandered away from the light crystals and into the dark woods after some food. He cocked his pebble gun and walked quietly on the silvery dead leaves that covered the forest floor. A flurry of wind distracted him and then he grew curious. There was a hole in the rock before him, and he slid himself in, into darkness, into the tunnel.

Then there was cold and pain and a metamorphosis ... and then there was 2111, unnamed now except for a prime number, unmarked except for the pain of change. Even his pack, far away, would not recognize him now, the way the Mytro pulled him like taffy through its darkness and left him a slave.

Perhaps 2111 could get more Nayzun out? Maybe 411 was the beginning of an exodus. Maybe the prisoners could go back to their homes, their families. Maybe he could get back to hunting, to sleeping by the light crystals, curled around his babies for protection.

Maybe the Nayzun could escape?

But now the Mytro didn't allow anyone to escape. The Nayzuns couldn't enter the stations anymore, only the tunnels, and they couldn't interact with humans on the trains. How much the Mytro knew about their whereabouts was still uncertain - after all, 411 had hidden a human in the new hangar and then interacted with humans without the Mytro knowing - but there was a good chance that the system knew more than it was letting on. After all, synchronicity was the root of power.

2111 still had a few tunnels to repair. He felt the humans riding the Mytro around him and narrowly avoided falling under the tracks of a line going between New York and London. The humans were using the Mytro more often now, since the children had closed the Breach. More use meant more abuse. More abuse meant an angrier Mytro.

Then there was the Builder who was doing some strange things. She was getting closer to the hangar, and it would be only a matter of time before she began meddling in affairs she didn't understand.

Perhaps, thought the Nayzun, *the Mytro will let us go if we prevent the humans from ruining things again.* It seemed like a sound plan. He could keep the humans out, convince them not to use the trains anymore, and keep the Nayzun free and the Mytro happy.

But 2111 didn't trust the Mytro to keep its side of the bargain. So he would fight, fight like he once fought on his own planet. And he would win.

CHAPTER TWELVE

Sushi

Agata and Maya left school early. The principal knew that Maya had an internship and Agata called her mother to say she was feeling sick and was excused. She wouldn't have much time to meet Mr. Kincaid - she'd have to rush to the station and then home – but she needed to see what was going on. She needed to find out what Kincaid was up to, why he wanted to meet.

Mr. Kincaid had met the children when they first discovered the Mytro. He had posed as a friend of her father, but in reality, he was working with the Mytratti to steal her father's Key - the object that could, for a time, control the Mytro. It allowed the owner to become a Builder, someone who could imagine a station and it would appear. It turned the owner into part of the Mytro.

Mr. Kincaid had disappeared after Agata and Turtle shut down the Breach but now he was back. Was he still a Mytratti? All Agata knew was that he was responsible for the disappearance of her father. And she was going to make him pay.

But there was Maya. What would she do with her? She couldn't bring her into the Mytro, but she could use the help. She would need the help if she was going to find her father. Could she bring her for a minute, just as backup? If something bad happened, Maya could run and tell someone. That way Agata wouldn't be alone.

She decided to text Turtle. He'd be able to help. She wasn't afraid to face Kincaid, but they had been a team since they started, always having each other's backs.

They exited the school and stood blinking in the Mediterranean sun. The sky was a deep blue, and a scud of clouds, rough at the edges, was coming in from the sea. It was warm but not hot, and the street was quiet in this less populated district of Barcelona.

They walked a bit. Maya bought a Fanta but Agata didn't want one.

Angre rose up inside her at the thought of Kincaid.

This was the man who had kidnapped her father. The man who nearly killed them. Now he wanted to apologize? She thought for a minute, prepared herself. She would meet him. But she needed backup.

"Maya, I need to show you something. It's dangerous. You don't have to come with me if you don't want to," said Agata.

"What is it?"

"It's something pretty crazy. And I need you to stay calm."

Maya, a girl who was surprisingly good at being the loudest one in the gym, was rarely calm. But she pursed her lips for a moment and nodded. "Sure. Calm. So what's up?"

Agata's Mytro stop was a block from the school down a small street, inside a deep vestibule built into an apartment building erected in 1928. It had the strange lines of a gothic cathedral, all curves and sea monsters etched into rich white stone, and right off the door, next to the mailboxes, was a hidden Mytro station.

She pushed a part of the wall and it seemed to fall inward, a gust of wind blowing about the both of them as it moved. The gust pulled them in, their hair and sweaters caught in the swirl, and Maya and Agata were suddenly both inside.

"Agata?" Maya gasped and looked around. The station was made of smooth concrete with old stonework embedded in it. It looked like an old building rebuilt by conservators. A row of five small gargoyles stood above the main door, which was made of rough banded wood. Agata always wondered who built this little station. It looked newer than the rest and had only been up on the 13 app a few months prior. Before she found this one, she had used another station, farther from school, that was hidden in the basement of a tapas bar.

"There are things in the universe that we don't quite understand, right?" Agata asked.

"Right," said Maya slowly.

"Well, this is one of the biggest and weirdest. You know how Turtle shows up every few days? He lives in New York. He takes a train to see us every time. It only takes a few seconds to get from Brooklyn to Barcelona."

"Are you serious? Can we go to Japan?" asked Maya.

"We can go anywhere, but first, we need to go meet someone. This is a dangerous guy and I don't like him. If anything happens, I need you to run and call the police."

"Agata, are you crazy?"

"I wish I were. But once I show you what's going on here, you're going to have a lot of fun."

"So Tokyo. We can go to Tokyo?" asked Maya.

"Sure."

"But first we go find a guy who's trying to kill you. Then we can have sushi."

"Pretty much," said Agata, smiling for the first time that day.

CHAPTER THIRTEEN

The Hammer

Someone was knocking on the old man's door. They knocked three times, each tap echoing in the hollow hangar like thunder. Little Bit woke with a start. The old man sniffled and stretched. Little Bit barked.

He looked at his watch. Almost eight in the morning. How did anyone get past the heavy front door? Did they buzz? He hadn't had a working buzzer in years. Three more knocks.

"Mr. Ioli, it's us," said a voice, muffled through the heavy door. It was a British accent, plummy.

"Us who?" he croaked. He needed a glass of water, so he stood and turned to the sink on the wall, taking an old mug down from his little shelf and letting the water run a little. He wouldn't open his door for anyone, least of all people who were playing funny games.

"The people who are paying for you to live here," said the voice.

This was a surprise. He had never met the people paying him. They paid him fifty thousand dollars in cash for the apartment (a price that, in retrospect, had been far too low), which they had changed into this hangar, somehow. And they paid him monthly to live there, all of it deposited into his checking account.

They paid for his silence.

He had once worked with a man, Richie "the Hammer" Barr. They called him "the Hammer" because he was good at putting guys down in the street.

He was a bouncer at a place that the old man used to frequent, when he was much younger, and this Hammer guy had connections all over Brooklyn and around the world. It was the Hammer who told him about the deal.

The old man remembered the day. He remembered the day things changed, a decade before.

When the old man wasn't so old but wasn't so young, after the old man's wife died and he bought Little Bit for company, the Hammer came to visit. They sat in his sunny front parlor, facing each other. There was black crepe on a picture of his wife on the table in front of him.

The Hammer sat down, his bulk filling the old couch, the horsehair underneath groaning with his weight. The Hammer sighed.

"Barry, my man, how are you?"

The old man, Bernard Ioli, nodded. "Good. Could be better."

The old man didn't like being called Barry, but he didn't dare correct the Hammer.

The Hammer looked over at the picture of Mr. Ioli's wife. She was beautiful – petite, with a heart-shaped face and dark hair. Mr. Ioli remembered putting his face in that hair, the perfume of it. He remembered her every day. Now she was gone.

"She was lovely lady. Truly. My sorrow. I never got married and maybe that's for the best, right?"

The Hammer spoke English funny, like he learned it late. Mr. Ioli nodded again.

"Look, we have a proposal. It's something big. We're looking for someone to help out."

"What is it?"

The Hammer explained that it was a refurb job, that they would change his apartment. He'd live there rent-free forever. The owner of the building would see to everything. There would be no more rent checks, and he'd get money every month for doing nothing.

"We're near a retirement, Barry. We all need a little something," said the Hammer.

The old man nodded, his head bobbing. Little Bit snoozed on the couch, snuffling lightly, barking in her sleep.

Mr. Ioli looked around the room. "Remodeling?"

"Remodeling. This would all be different. Completely different. You just keep place safe. Tell us if someone comes."

A week later the Hammer came back. He brought a few men with him, men in trench coats who spoke something that sounded like Spanish but wasn't. They wheeled in a large crate, about as big as a door, with the words "Fragile" and "This Side Up" painted on it.

"Portuguese," said the Hammer. "These boys are contractors."

Mr. Ioli looked at their hands. They were thin and pale with manicured nails. One wore a large white watch with a gold case and leather band, which he kept checking as they spoke.

"Those aren't contractors," said Mr. Ioli. "Where are their tools?"

"Go take walk, Barry. This won't take long," said the Hammer.

The men led him out of his apartment, and he took Little Bit up the street to Sunset Park, back down the other side and past Green-Wood Cemetery. He passed a bar that he used to frequent before he was married and pulled up a barstool. He had a beer, then two.

It was warm the day the Portuguese men came, and Mr. Ioli walked out into the afternoon sun and smiled, light and free, thanks to two beers and then two more. He looked down at Little Bit, who looked up at him with interest. He had a little money, now, and whatever they were doing in the house wouldn't last long. Wise guys like the Hammer usually worked in the short-term. As long as it wasn't illegal, he was OK with it. They passed a deli.

"Ham sandwich?"

Little Bit wagged her tail. Mr. Ioli bought two, one for him and one for Little Bit. They finished them on the way home.

When he got back, it wasn't home anymore. The Portuguese men were gone, and the Hammer was sitting on a chair, his face pale, almost green.

"Hey, buddy. I'm glad you're back," he said. "So we've got a little problem..."

That was ten years ago. Now different men were back.

Little Bit barked twice, her little voice echoing in the huge hangar that was now Mr. Ioli's home. The Hammer never came back, after that, and no one ever told him what he was supposed to do besides live his life and be quiet. He had sold his silence and bought loneliness – a decade of loneliness.

Whoever it was knocked on the door again.

"Mr. Ioli. It's us. We're here to help you put your life back on track," said the British voice again. "Should that be what you want to do."

Mr. Ioli put down the mug on the sink, walked to the door, and twisted back the deadbolt.

CHAPTER FOURTEEN

Slice by Slice

s the ghost rode Mark down the crowded Brooklyn avenue, shoppers jostled the ghost on its way up, and the ghost marveled at how humans felt. It had been centuries since he had been human and being next to this one was new and sharp and clear. The Nayzun shell he once wore was comfortable and powerful but it didn't allow for much freedom. Colors weren't as vibrant, smells were muted, and sounds were muffled. Speaking without speaking was convenient, but to be in his old slave body, stuck there by the Mytro, was a crime against nature and the ghost had rebelled and escaped. Now he was back on a human, even if for a short time, and it felt good.

The ghost remembered the transition into his Nayzun body. The Mytro, he realized too late, was a trap, a dark hole into which things fell and kept falling, never coming back. The men and women who fell into it - and there were thousands - were thrown into an endless darkness for what seemed like years. Once the body was shorn away – a process that the ghost remembered as intensely painful, akin to being shaved slice by slice – only the consciousness remained. The Mytro poured that consciousness into the Nameless Ones, bodies bred long ago to be the perfect worker. Then it was simply a process of forgetting – forgetting first the pain, then the identity, then the humanity. All his years as a Nayzun had protected him from sadness and fear, and now, in this human body, he found those feelings returning.

"Are you well?" asked Mark from inside himself.

I am sad. It has been a long time since I was sad.

The ghost knew he wasn't the only kind of being trapped in a Nayzun body. The Mytro ran everywhere, and creatures that no man could even imagine were trapped in its tunnels. Those were the quieter Nayzun, the ones who stayed together in the hangar, clinging to the faint memory of their shared existence, like hungry people clinging to the scent of bread. Human Nayzun were harder to control and more solitary, each living in their own horror.

But no matter what they had been, they all longed to be free at first ... and soon gave up. They all struggled at first, fought the sense that the Mytro was the Alpha and the Omega, the beginning and the end. But something about being trapped in the Nayzun body calmed the soul. The Nayzun body did not grow, did not get hungry, took sustenance from the air and the dark. It was delightfully efficient but horribly inhuman.

But now the ghost was free. And the ghost had some business to attend to.

The ghost spoke. *There is a Breach in a building ahead. I do not know where, but I can try to lead you to it as best I can. My senses aren't as strong as they were.*

Mark grunted, wondering what all of this meant, but he was happy to help. Excited, in fact. In his years as a monk, he had felt peace, but he had never felt a world outside the mundane one of cooking smells, incense, and street noise. He had always wanted proof of the spirit world but was afraid to ask.

"What are you?" Mark asked under his breath, as he passed a woman carrying two orange sacks of groceries. The woman looked up, confused, and kept walking.

I am a man, or I was. What happened to me could happen to many others if we are not careful. We are trying to solve a riddle, monk, and I need someone with hands and feet to help me.

"So you are a soul?"

If it helps you to think that way, yes, I am.

Mark nodded slightly. "Please do not hurt anyone," he said.

I can't. Only you can, with your hands.

Mark felt the ghost shiver on his back. They were in front of a building that Mark didn't recognize. Trash cans were carefully hidden in an alcove next to the front door and the number 13 was spray-painted in faded black near the door. A barred, shaded window looked out on the street next to the red door.

It is here.

Mark walked to the front door. It was made of steel, painted and repainted over the years so it looked like mottled leather. There were six apartments, and Mark scanned the names written on fly-specked cards displayed behind dirty glass.

A little man in a bowler hat and bow tie approached the door behind him.

This man is a friend, said the ghost, and Mark turned to him, feeling a surge of recognition, as if the ghost were telling him who to trust.

"Hello. I think you and I have a mutual acquaintance," said Mark. The little man started and looked into Adam's eyes, then past him, at the red door.

"Wonderful. Who might that be? I'm Mr. Partridge by the way," said the little man, holding out a small, dry hand. "And you are?"

CHAPTER FIFTEEN

Dark Letter

s Lionel was lifting one of the heavy pods off the stamper, his phone buzzed with an incoming text, and he almost dropped the metal. Claude cursed as the heavy shell fell back into the mold.

"Eyes on the prize, how you say," said Claude.

Lionel nodded.

"Sorry dude. Important call."

He pulled out a black phone that he had purchased online. It was supposed to be completely secure and uncrackable, and he used it to communicate with a secure messaging system with his programmer friends. Now one of them was texting him.

Hello. Are you making the pods?

Who is this? Lionel texted back.

I'd rather not say. We have an operative in your area who may come by to see you and explain to you what you are building. Those pods are very dangerous.

Lionel thought about showing Claude and Pawel the texts but decided not to.

Tell me who this is, he texted back.

He put his phone in his pocket to help Claude pull off the sheet of metal then dropped it with a clang on the floor. A different number texted.

Hello. Sorry for the secrecy. I'll explain who I am when I arrive. I'm British. My name is Partridge. I'll be there after I visit another site. You are building graves.

Graves. The word chilled him. Graves?

Lionel looked at the pods. They were big enough to hold a human. He hadn't thought of that before - or maybe he had and had put it out of his mind. When he built things, especially things that held people, he always worked towards comfort and safety. These would be comfortable, perhaps womb-like.

But there were no air holes, no way for those inside to breathe.

"Guys," said Lionel, "I think we have a problem."

CHAPTER SIXTEEN

This Is Your End

Mr. Ioli opened the door. Two men stood before him, one tall and lean with thick glasses, the other smaller, fatter, and bald with red splotches on his face. They both wore heavy wool coats, cold came off them in waves, as if they had just come from someplace where it was winter. Mr. Ioli shivered.

They were not the Portuguese men. They were from somewhere else, somewhere farther away. They looked like men on a long journey.

"Hello," said the short man. "I'm Mr. Goode. And this is Mr. Adams. I presume you're Mr. Ioli?"

Mr. Ioli grunted.

"A pleasure, sir, a true pleasure. We've heard so much about you – you're now the stuff of legend in our line of work. A hired man who did what was asked, who went above and beyond, and who followed his instructions to the letter. We're now the owners of this building and we'd like to introduce ourselves to the tenants. We came to you first, though, even though you're at the top of the stairs. You're our most prized tenant."

"I don't remember Richie saying anything about you two. It's been a long time," said Mr. Ioli. "I only know two fellas from Portugal. You aren't them."

"I know those two. They are no longer with our firm but no matter. If it's a question of documentation, I'm sure we can provide with signatures and bank statements that will show our regular payments to you in hopes of allowing you some comfort in your advanced age. But where are my manners? If I recall correctly, your name is Bernard? Bernard Ioli?" asked the Mr. Goode.

"Bernie. Yes," said Mr. Ioli.

"Bernie, may we come in?" asked Mr. Adams as he put his body into the doorway. He looked up and over the fake wall and at the dark ceiling high above. He whistled, a rush of air between his lips like a tea kettle warming up.

"There's nowhere to sit," said Mr. Ioli.

"We'll stand," said Mr. Goode.

The two walked into the room and Mr. Ioli closed the door behind them. Little Bit was up and excited. She hadn't had visitors in years. She waggled her hind legs like a puppy, squealing a little and yipping. Mr. Adams reached down to pet her on the back. She was sick now, too old, and getting skinnier. Mr. Adams ran a large finger over her vertebrae, the bones knotted and hard under her thin fur and pink skin. Little Bit squeaked once and moved her head under the big man's hand until his thumb and forefinger found the back of her small ears and rubbed her there gently.

"How old is the dog?" asked Mr. Adams.

"Two years older than this place," said Mr. Ioli. Little Bit looked at him through rheumy eyes, grunting a little as Mr. Adams worked his magic. "Not the building, but this room."

"She's a good one," said Mr. Adams. "Not many dogs are this friendly."

Mr. Ioli didn't want to sit on his bed even though his knees were hurting. He didn't want them to hulk over him like so many younger people did over the old.

"You two look like you're here to collect something," said Mr. Ioli.

"We are, in a way, but not from you," said Mr. Goode. "Your employer of all these years is dead. He died two years ago, and we only just now learned of this place and his unique set of skills. He was one of the Portuguese men you met so long ago. His property is now our property and we've taken over his debts and his obligations. This place is one of them and your employment is another."

Mr. Goode walked around, marveling at the space.

"Impressive," he said. "This was built for a very specific purpose and then forgotten. You were tasked with protecting it, I understand, and you have done an exemplary job. We are offering you a few possible rewards for your long service. You'll have a few moments to make a decision, but I assure you there won't be much to think about. We are very fair – and very convincing – men."

These two men seem more like wise guys, like a strange, British version of Richie the Hammer, thought the old man. He had never asked questions and never explored the hangar to its edges, even though, for two years, the thought of what could be hidden in the deep dark was frightening. He imagined ghosts or monsters or dead men desiccating in the cave-like space, but he was a grown man and too old for ghosts.

He suspected now that he might have just met the monsters.

"You see, this is a sort of magical place. You knew that, in your heart, but it never made sense, I suspect?" asked Mr. Goode.

"What do you mean?" asked Mr. Ioli.

"There's no sane reason you should be living inside a 100,000-square-meter apartment, even in Brooklyn," said Mr. Goode. "Yet here you are. The idea for this place was for it to be a gathering spot for a new project that was started long before you and I were born. It was an interesting effort, to be sure, and whoever built it a decade ago knew what they were doing. And they clearly knew a good caretaker when they saw one, Mr. Ioli."

"But this place is only a decade old. They changed it over after my wife died, when they started paying me," said the old man.

"The place, as it exists now, has existed for a century. It was a gathering spot long ago. The Portuguese men, in essence, moved it to your location, or at least the location you used to call your apartment. It takes a lot of power to do that, but they did it for you because they trusted you. They trusted you not to talk and to take good care of it," said Mr. Goode. "And you did just that."

"Why did I need to be here? Why couldn't they build it and just let me be?"

"It was built using a very specific technique. Remember the old riddle, 'If a tree falls in the forest and there's no one around to hear it, does it make a sound?' It's like that. If you weren't here, there would be a sort of shift in the room and it would have gone away ... or worse. In fact, no one was sure that it would even survive with you inside it. It was very unstable. You were the lone witness. I know it doesn't sound very nice nor was it terribly convenient for you."

"So that's it? You leave me here for a decade and then I'm supposed to leave? This is my home," said Mr. Ioli. He thought about the tree in the forest and then shuddered. If what this British man was saying was true, then the entire room could have collapsed in on him by some power he did not see nor understand. He had been sitting on a powder keg.

"That's our question now, Mr. Ioli, and we think we can come to an amicable conclusion. Bernie ..." Mr. Goode said again, exhaling the word like a prayer. "What do we do with Bernie?"

CHAPTER SEVENTEEN

Kincaids

"You still suck, Turd-le," whispered Nate Kincaid. The teacher, who had been drawing an advanced trigonometry problem on the board, turned around and looked at Turtle who had turned in his seat to face Nate.

"Mr. Fulton, you seem bored," said his teacher, Mrs. Paolini. "Perhaps you can solve this for us?"

"Yes, ma'am," said Turtle as he felt his face grow hot. He figured he had turned red. Mrs. Paolini had surprised him, but he deserved it. He had been daydreaming a moment before, thinking of his London run and what Mr. Partridge had said about the Mytratti.

Now he turned away from the sneering Nate and took stock of the situation. The board was full of notations and graphs, but in a few seconds he understood it perfectly and stood up and walked to the board. Taking an erasable marker from Mrs. Paolini, he started in, chomping down the math problem until it was complete. He was good at math and most of this was easy for him. He added a few lines to the problem and then got into it in earnest, the burning in his face replaced by concentration.

Nate and Turtle used to be friends but that stopped when their uncle had disappeared. They blamed Turtle, and Turtle didn't know how to explain what had happened. Mr. Partridge had recommended not explaining anything at all, even though the twins knew about the Mytro. Whatever they knew was not enough to make them understand what had happened in the Breach, what their uncle had done and how horribly he had acted. Besides, he had no idea where their uncle went. When they closed the Breach, he had disappeared, and the Conductor's Guild believed he was still working for the Mytratti. No one had heard from him in months, and Turtle had no way to tell Nick and Nate where he had gone.

The truth was that Mr. Kincaid had turned on Turtle and Agata in Barcelona and then run, and it seemed that Mr. Kincaid hadn't told anyone where he went. He had just hid, leaving the Kincaid family a mess.

"We never should have told you about the Mytro, you idiot," said Nate on the day after Mr. Kincaid disappeared. Turtle wanted to tell the twins about how they were duped, how their uncle had worked with a bad man to essentially enslave a group of poor people, but how could he? They wouldn't believe him. Turtle almost didn't believe it himself.

And so. his friendship with Nick and Nate was done. Even Nick, the twin who showed Turtle how to board his first train, froze him out and didn't want anything to do with him. Nate, on the other hand, was actively mean, pushing Turtle's books out of his arms in between classes and trying to trip him ... which was what Nate did now as Turtle returned to his desk.

Turtle sidestepped the leg and Nate slipped, sliding over to one side. His books smacked onto the floor and his desk nearly flipped, leaving Nate sputtering on the floor.

The teacher turned to look and Nate muttered something about slipping. He righted his desk and Turtle sat down behind him.

Turtle wanted to be friends with the twins, to introduce them to Agata and the Conductor's Guild, and to tell them about the Mytratti and all the trouble they caused. But he couldn't. He didn't dare. And he wasn't sure why he was so scared.

These days he didn't need Nick or Nate, really. He had made other friends that year and was able to stay out of Nick and Nate's way. He had introduced his friend Oz Kneen to the Mytro but reminded Oz to stay only on the tunnels and stops he knew and not to travel outside the network. The twins were upset that Turtle and Oz used the Mytro station under the school, but they had stopped locking the door on them after the janitor, Mr. Goudas, had asked for a camera to watch the downstairs door, a request that was never granted.

From his seat behind Nate in trig class, Oz now mimed smacking the twin in the head. Turtle shook his head no. It wasn't worth a fight, especially now.

The bell rang, and Oz and Turtle went out into the hall. Nate stayed behind.

"That was intense. What happened?" asked Oz.

"He tried to trip me and then he lost his balance. I didn't hit him at all," said Turtle. "Or, well ... maybe a little bit with my hip. But it was totally accidental."

Oz nodded, slowly, smiling.

"Very nice. What's your plan today?" asked Oz.

"I think I need to go to Brooklyn after school," said Turtle. "My friend needs help."

"I'll come with you," said Oz, a tall, lanky basketball player.

Oz and Turtle had bonded over their affinity for Minecraft and spent a few hours every weekend or so playing together on a massive network. Turtle liked the game because it reminded him of how the Mytro stations worked – he could build them in any shape he wanted, with just the power of thought. After discovering the Mytro, Turtle rarely played games anymore - there didn't seem to be any need when the world was truly an adventure - but it was fun to hang with Oz.

Even though Oz knew about the Mytro and even had his own limited copy of the map, he didn't like to ride it. He said it made him feel creepy to go into the dark. Some days, however, they'd both ride around Manhattan together, ending up in Brooklyn in a wink and then rolling into Union Square in the city after picking up chicken sandwiches at their favorite place near Prospect Park. They'd eat the sandwiches in the park, and then Turtle would ride with him to Oz's house in Queens and then ride home. They called those "Chicken Sandwich Days."

"Meet me downstairs after school. I don't have track practice," said Turtle. "I'm thinking it's a Chicken Sandwich Day after I meet my friend."

"Great. I'll be ready right after. Basketball's cancelled because Mr. Goudas pulled something," said Oz. "So yes, CSD."

"Perfect," said Turtle. Oz raised his hand for a high five, and Turtle, smirking, gave him one. After years of quiet trips down the hall, it felt good to have a friend. The Mytro had helped him grow, that much was sure, and having Agata as a friend, even if she was in Barcelona, was great as well.

The next periods went by slowly. He had history - they were studying the colonization of India by the British - and then English where they were reading *Moby Dick*. He nearly nodded off as the early morning miles in London caught up with him, but he forced himself to stay awake and pay attention. The best way to keep a secret was to make it look like you didn't have time to keep a secret, he had decided, so along with his world travel, he had begun working harder in school.

He was in the hall when his phone buzzed. He looked down at it, curious. It was a message from Agata.

Need to meet. Urgent. 10 minutes in Madrid. Under Lucifer. Don't approach. Stay back and hide.

Mysterious! Are you OK? he sent back.

The three dots that meant she was sending a message blinked and then he read, *I think so. I need your help. Can't explain now.*

"Under Lucifer" meant the statue of Lucifer, the only one of the fallen angel in the world. It was in the Retiro Park, a beautiful rolling space that Agata and Turtle liked to walk through on weekends. It was also their emergency spot. If he left now, he'd be back by the time the next bell rang. He rushed through the hall toward the basement stairs.

The students at Manhattan Friends had rolled out into the halls and their voices mingled into a roar. It was Turtle's lunch time – 11:00 a.m. - and freshmen were being knocked over while the upperclassmen joked and talked, quietly, about going to concerts in the city as they approached the school exit. The jazz band started tuning up – they could be heard even on the top floor - and the tennis team was practicing in the gym.

Turtle heard the *toc tocs* of balls and the *thwack* of rackets as he moved in the opposite direction, heading for the basement where the locker rooms and boiler room were, as well as the music rooms and computer lab and the outdoor sports locker rooms. It was darker down there, quieter, and the bright fluorescents could barely break the gloom in the long hallway that led to the back of the school. Someone had said this was the oldest part of the building, built in the 1800s. It felt like it.

Oz was waiting for him in the locker room. The track and basketball teams weren't practicing, and the football team had taken a yellow bus to an away game. The basement was empty.

"I saw you head down here," he said. "What's up?"

"Nothing, Oz. Not a big deal," said Turtle. "I just have to go somewhere."

"Then I'm coming," said Oz.

Turtle looked down at his phone and then at his friend. "Fine, but we have to hurry," said Turtle.

"I already ate so we don't even have to grab lunch," said Oz. He was excited to get out of school, even for forty-five minutes.

They passed through the locker room to the boiler room. In the back room, the boiler was cold and the room smelled of oil and dust. They snuck quietly between the tall metal lockers, the smell of sweat and rotten sports gear melding into something as stark as gasoline fumes. It was oddly calming, however. This was Turtle's way in and out, his secret entrance.

"OK. We need alibis. This might take a while. Go," said Turtle.

Oz texted his parents and said he would stay over at Turtle's. Turtle texted his grandmother and told her he would stay over at Oz's.

The Mytro station was behind the boiler and was accessed by pressing on a certain brick, blackened by the handprints of countless kids. Turtle looked around as they waited for the door to open. They were alone. The door fell inward, quietly, on invisible hinges. As they stepped into the small station, a wind blared up and slammed the door behind them.

The train roared into the station a moment later, right on time. It wasn't a modern train. It had a gas headlight and consisted of two long cars coupled together. They were painted a deep crimson that was almost brown and had black-iron front and back platforms. Two red lights blinked on the burnished copper roof, and the front and back of each sloped gently down, making the train look almost like a centipede. The wheels rattled against the rails as it stopped, and the cars heaved forward, then settled on their springs as the doors - two on each car - swung back and in, hissing compressed air as they swung. Another hiss of air signaled that the brakes had let go. The train sat idling on the tracks.

Oz gasped. It was great to see him happy.

Then Oz screamed.

CHAPTER TWENTY

Shell and Green Skin

2111 unfolded as it came onto the platform from the gloom at the end of the tunnel. It was a tall, thin creature with long legs and arms, and there were dents where its eyes would be and small holes where ears would be and no mouth. It spoke somehow, though, and the boys heard its wheezing breath. It had long, thin fingers, and its skin was almost pearlescent. To Oz it looked like a cross between a ghost and an alien. He raced to the back of the room and tried the door. It was locked. Turtle turned to him, his hand out, motioning for calm.

"Chill, Oz. We're OK."

The Nayzun rose to his full height. As the crown of his head touched the ceiling of the station, it brushed down a little rain of dust.

Are you the boy? The boy with the Key?

Oz heard the voice in his head. It was the sound of clashing brakes, of electricity running down a long track. It was energy in the dark, massing, ebbing, and flowing into distant junctures. It was the sound of accidents on a snowy pass, of fear and hollow voices heard from under snow. It was wild and full of wind.

But Turtle answered, "I'm Paul Fulton. They call me Turtle. I have a Key."

2111 thought for a moment. Was that the name? He had heard of turtles before but this child did not look like those things. The thing humans called *turtle* had shells and green skin.

Turtle?

"It's a nickname, like your name. You're a prime number now, but you had a real name. Long ago."

2111 was again confused. There was no fear in this boy, and the boy seemed to know more about 2111 than anyone. Perhaps this boy knew his real name? Perhaps that was a power he had?

The Nayzun shuddered as it shrunk a little. The tall boy who screamed was slowly returning, wary. The smaller boy, the turtle, was brave and tall.

Are you the boy I seek?

"I am, I think. Who sent you? What is your name?"

2111 had come of his own volition. He had heard about the boy and the girl from the man in the water, and he had hidden this information from the Mytro for months - months of human time at least. 2111 once thought the Mytro knew everything. Now, after months of hiding the human in the water, 2111 knew that wasn't true. The Mytro was losing its grip and it was going mad. And it was time for the boy and his friend to help.

I am 2111. I came on my own. We need your help.

"What do you mean?" asked Turtle.

There is too much death. My people are being killed. They are being burnt alive every day. The Mytro is angry. It wants to hurt us ... and you too.

"I'm sorry," said Turtle. "I didn't know about that. How can we help?"

A man is going to the Breach. He is in danger. We are in danger. I know what you did for 411. I need you to do it for all of us.

"All of you?" asked Turtle, shivering a little, thinking about what had been asked of him.

Everyone in the hangar. There can't be any more Nameless Ones. We want to return to our homes, to know our real names. We want freedom.

"That means you die," said Turtle.

Then that's what we want.

"Where are the others? Do they know about your plan?"

With your assistance, I am sure we can convince more to help us. We have nothing to lose. We are the basis for your devils. We are the basis for your demons. Men who have seen us fear us, but we know we were once men. Help us, the turtle. We want to be rid of all that.

Turtle nodded while Oz shook his head.

We must also stop the humans from making new Nayzun if we ever want to escape.

Turtle looked up at the Nayzun quizzically.

The Nayzun are made, not bornThe way to build the population is to take lifeforms and change them. I was changed, as was 411. We still remember a little of our old lives, but as we age, we forget so much.

But the Mytro needs Nayzun. Entire cultures have sacrificed their beings to the Mytro in order to gain a little power. The Mytro doesn't eat these beings in the way you imagine, but it uses their life force to bolster itself. Humans were the only ones who were able to create Keys, tools that could tame the Mytro without sacrifice, which is why the Mytro has been trapping beings far from Earth to populate the stations here. But the Mytratti are attempting to flood the Mytro with humans. They are making strange promises.

"So they're stealing humans?"

I don't know. I can't understand their actions, only the results. I believe they are gathering people in major cities though. Your London is the first spot.

"So you want us to stop them and free all of you ... so the Mytro starves?" asked Turtle.

The Nayzun hummed lightly, a sound like wind against a glass window.

Oz smiled despite his fear. Turtle turned to him and coughed, thinking about how to explain things to him.

"A few months ago we met some men. They wanted to capture hundreds of refugees and make them work in these tunnels, probably making things. T-shirts, electronics, that kind of stuff. They were basically going to hide an entire workforce out of sight. We stopped them," said Turtle.

"You did?" asked Oz.

"It was harder than it sounds. So what this guy here is saying is they're trying again. We need to figure out what they're doing and how they're doing it. But we need some help." Turtle turned then to the Nayzun. "OK. We're going to get to the bottom of this, 2111, but we've got to go now. How can we find you?"

I can hear you on the rails. I'll find you when you need me.

"Good. See what you can learn and we'll meet up later tonight."

Time has no meaning to me. I will await you.

Oz's mouth was hanging open, so Turtle closed it for him.

"This is crazy," he said.

Turtle just shrugged and smiled. "You get used to it," he said. A train rolled into the station and the Nayzun moved to let them pass. They boarded the train and it clattered into the dark.

CHAPTER TWENTY-ONE

The Red Door

dam's hand was frozen in Mr. Partridge's, and he was now staring off into the distance. The ghost was trying to take control and Mark didn't want to let it or, more correctly, didn't know how to let it. It felt like a cough stuck in his throat only more urgent.

"My boy, are you quite alright?"

Suddenly there was a break and Mark let the ghost through. It was like ripping open a present – the surprise greater than the result. Mark relaxed. The ghost spoke.

Why are you here, Partridge? asked Mark, with the Nayzun speaking through him.

"Fascinating. 4-1-1, I presume?" said Mr. Partridge, speaking the numbers one by one: four – one – one. A prime.

In a manner of speaking, yes. We must leave here.

"We must, but first I must understand this. You say you're that chap there? Or you are inside him?"

The Nayzun bodies were created long ago. The bodies we were forced into when we captured by the Mytro are little more than machines that, in their own way, shape the mind of the being within them. Like the water takes the shape of the vase, once captured, we took the shape of the Nayzun.

But being freed gave me a new ability to move from being to being. I could take you, if I wished, but this man has been kind enough to loan himself for at least this brief period. I worried that if I couldn't talk to you, you wouldn't understand the import of what was happening. You cannot go through that door. Not yet.

"I see," said Mr. Partridge. "This sounds dire."

The Nayzun have long known of the Breach behind that door. The men that control it, men you know, are very dangerous. They will not let you interfere with their project.

"How do you know?"

We Nayzun protected another human from them, Ernesto Llorente. I understand he is a distant relation of mine, but I cannot tell exactly how we are connected, only that we have a bond. We put him into hiding to protect him from those who would find him, especially the Mytro itself.

"So the Mytro stands to benefit? Why would the Mytro care?"

Because these men are bringing it more Nayzun.

Mr. Partridge paused. It all made sense. The Guild had suspected as much all along. But they never had proof. It would be a busy but enlightening day. In fact, thought, Mr. Partridge, he could avoid a great deal of fuss if everything went well during his visits.

The ghost left Mark for a moment and the monk seemed to shrivel slightly, as if exhausted. He grunted softly. Mr. Partridge smiled.

"How do you do?" asked Mr. Partridge cheerfully. He was in his element. "I assume this isn't the Nayzun?"

"I think so. I'm Mark Lao and this has been a strange afternoon," he said, smiling wanly and wiping his brow. He had suddenly broken out in a cold sweat.

"I'm Lionel Partridge. I'm a researcher. I think you're exceedingly lucky. I've never seen this sort of thing on the Mytro, but you are – it can be told – in very good hands with the being that is inhabiting you. I wonder if you can explain what exactly you feel?"

"It's like a cold bath and then I can't move. The ghost moves everything for me. If you relax, it's not so bad, but if you struggle, it becomes horrible. I think my meditation has helped me handle the transitions," said Mark.

"An excellent observation. I think that is the case as well. You should know that you are being ridden by what is known as a Nameless One, a Nayzun. These are the souls, or perhaps the ghosts, of people who have been changed in a very real, fundamental way. They have been forced to toil for a very cruel, fickle master. The one that has taken you escaped and now requires humans to manifest itself. You are a vessel and it is steering. I hope you don't mind. I'm quite happy to invite the Nayzun into me if you are squeamish or upset."

"I'm not upset. It's just an odd feeling."

"It will, I suspect, get odder. Now, for the matter at hand. We are about to enter what is called a Breach. It is a break in the space continuum where strange things happen. If the ghost, as you call it, doesn't take you right away, then you will be quite disoriented. Please don't pay it any mind and understand that I'm here with you to help."

They entered the building and began climbing. Mark coughed and Mr. Partridge slapped him softly on the back. Then 411 came back. Mark croaked in the Nayzun's voice, his own voice caught in his throat.

Do not enter that place. Do not go in. The ghost was speaking through Mark again in a strident tone.

"But I must," said Mr. Partridge. "I have to report back on what's going on here. It's important."

Then I will help if I can. But please prepare for the worst.

"I always have," said Mr. Partridge.

CHAPTER TWENTY-TWO

Lucifer Down

Agata and Maya came out of the Mytro from a station hidden in the wall of the Palacio de Cristal. This building, built in 1887 to house flora and fauna from the New World, was empty now and a safe spot to disembark. The station was hidden behind a locked door that said "Keep Out Room 13" in Spanish and English. It was quiet here. Lunchtime wanderers were headed towards the avenues while tourists rarely visited the spot, choosing instead to loll on the stairs to the Retiro Pond with its beautiful fountains and food stands.

A single bird stopped singing when they came out of the station and then started again, full-throated.

Maya loved traveling on the Mytro and smiled broadly as they pushed the brush away and popped out, blinking in the bright afternoon.

"I still can't believe this is real," she said.

"You'll get used to it, but Maya, this is dangerous. I think you should stay back," she said as she checked her watch. Turtle would be here any moment.

"Look, whatever's happening, I can help. I'm fast, I have a cell phone, I know karate," said Maya. Standing with her hands on her hips, straight as an arrow, she added, "I'm Super Maya."

Despite herself, Agata smiled. "Fine. But stay close, Super Maya," she said.

Two minutes passed and Turtle and a tall boy - Oz, Agata remembered - tumbled out of the Mytro station and through the bushes. They stood confused for a minute then spotted the girls. Agata ran to hug Turtle, and Oz held out his hand.

"We've met," he said. "I think?"

Agata pushed his hand away and hugged him too.

"We met in Brooklyn," she said. "You brought us cheesecake."

Maya hugged Turtle and shook Oz's hand. "Your name is like from the book?" she asked. "The Wizard?"

"It's actually Oswald but I don't like it," said Oz. "So it's Oz."

"Oswaldo," said Maya, smiling, "in Spanish."

It was late afternoon in Madrid, and the sun was slowly rolling down the sky and casting red streaks through the trees surrounding the greenhouse.

"OK, introductions made," said Turtle. "What's up?"

"Kincaid," said Agata. She showed him the text and explained her plan. "He wants to talk, but I don't trust him," she said. "So we go through the park together and I break off and you watch from afar. If anything happens, we all come together and stop him. If everything's fine, then no one else comes out. That way, if it's a trap, we'll know. He's meeting us by Lucifer."

"Not a fan. Listen. First, I'm coming with you," said Turtle. "Agata, you and I will talk to Kincaid. Oz, Maya, you hang back."

"Lucifer?" asked Oz.

"You'll see. It's nuts," said Turtle.

They fell in line and headed south to the statue.

They could see it through the trees that lined the park. It was a striking statue made of blackened bronze. Set on high plinth, it loomed over the small pool and fountain below it. Called *Fuente del Ángel Caído*, or the *Fountain of the Fallen Angel*, it once was a central location for the Mytratti to meet. The station in its base was now closed, but it was so well-known - recorded in old histories of the Mytro and in popular lore - that everyone could find it.

Standing in front of it amid a group of school children was a ragged, thin man with long hair and a beard. Oz and Maya stayed back, watching from a stand of trees while Turtle and Agata approached the school group.

The bearded man saw them and smiled, which made Agata think of the angel falling.

"It's him," said Turtle.

"It's him," said Agata.

He opened his arms to them. It was Mr. Kincaid.

CHAPTER TWENTY-THREE

In Time

Mr. Ioli had a battery-powered turntable in a box by the front wall. Mr. Goode saw it and opened it, carefully, like a doctor opening his leather bag.

"This is an oldie," said Mr. Goode. "Does it work?"

Mr. Ioli nodded to a stack of 45 records in a pile by the bed, and Mr. Goode picked one up. Sly and the Family Stone. "In Time."

Mr. Goode turned on the turntable and the speaker began to hiss. He turned it down and placed the disc onto the player then slowly moved the tone arm to the grooves. The tinny sound of Sly's electronic percussion issued forth.

"Sounds a bit slow," said Mr. Goode.

Mr. Ioli was edging towards the door. Mr. Adams noticed.

"We all get a bit slow as we get older," said Mr. Ioli.

"Here is what we want, Bernie. We want this apartment back. You've been paid handsomely. You'll be living in a place of our choosing, out of the way, for a period until we can finish our work. You won't be able to come and go, but you'll be fed and you can bring your records..."

"Look, I don't know you. I know a man named Barr who put me in here and told me to stay put. I don't think I should leave unless you guys have some paperwork."

"We don't have paperwork, Bernie, because, as you can imagine, this sort of situation is highly unorthodox. We've been able to maintain it thus through sheer force of will, and your safety is guaranteed by the men who long ago put Mr. Barr in charge. The less you know about this, the better."

This is my home, Mr. Ioli thought. This hangar. He was supposed to watch it. He was supposed to stay. What about Little Bit? She was sick. He had to stay.

"How about you go and get me some information – like a deed or whatever – and some information on this place where we're going and maybe we can talk then. In this country you don't do anything without a signed warrant."

Mr. Goode smiled, gently, as if he were talking to a recalcitrant puppy.

"If you'll recall, Mr. Ioli, the concept of an apartment being bigger on the inside than the outside started with our own beloved Dr. Who. However, you're right. We should have more documentation. That said, we do not have said documentation right now, but we will produce it as necessary. If you'll just come with us, we'll be able to settle you in and explain everything in the process."

Bernie was stuck. He looked around the room. What was there to move anyway? The apartment was empty. If he had been smart, he would have put all sorts of things in there, pile things up into the darkness. He could have collected bikes and fixed them up and sold them. He could have collected cans. He could have brought TVs in to repair. But he never did. He had always been scared of a knock on the door and the arrival of an unwanted visitor.

And today the knock came through the apartment, echoing in the Breach.

And then there was another buzz. Bernie looked up, surprised, and Little Bit began to bark. Years of silence and suddenly he had two visitors. Bernie stood to answer it but Mr. Goode ticked his tongue.

"No no no," he said. "None of that. We're the only visitors that matter."

CHAPTER TWENTY-FOUR

Old Foes

M r. Kincaid carried a tan backpack with a sleeping bag attached by black straps and wore threadbare, dark-brown shorts and a black T-shirt. He was skinny – skeletal – a new man.

Agata and Turtle pulled back in fear. Agata reached out, grabbing Turtle's hand with a little pressure, telling him that she was getting ready to run.

"Please, don't be afraid," said Mr. Kincaid, holding out his hands, trying to calm them. His eyes looked tired, as if he hadn't been sleeping. His hair was grayer now.

They were in public. The school group was nearby as were their friends. They could run.

"I'm not a Mytratti. Not anymore. I need you to get a letter to my family, please, Turtle, and I can tell you something important. Agata, please, I'm trying to help. I've found your father."

Agata gasped.

Mr. Kincaid sat down on the fountain and invited Agata and Turtle to do the same. Turtle did, but Agata stood, still ready to run. Oz and Maya watched from the trees, pretending to be in conversation. Turtle looked at them and Oz raised an eyebrow. With the slightest of motions, Turtle mouthed "OK."

"Thank you for stopping a moment," said Mr. Kincaid. "I'm sorry for what I did. I truly am. Mr. Goode was very convincing, but now his organization is out of control. It consists of a series of psychopaths and hundreds of cultists.

I was taken in. I was lied to. To me, it looked like the only way to continue my research, but now I realize what was happening ... and Goode is hungry for power in any form. He is consumed by that hunger. I didn't see it because I was consumed by my research."

"That's ridiculous," said Agata. "Research doesn't turn you into a bad person. My father was a good man. He studied the Mytro."

"This was my life's work. There is something about the Mytro. Something that pulls you in. Before I met you two, before I knew you had the Keys, I was researching space travel via the Mytro," said Mr. Kincaid. "Goode had said he had nearly perfected it - he just needed your Key, or so he told me. Truth is, he didn't know what he needed. He had no rigor. He took very basic ideas and carried them to their conclusions. He was not a thinker, and none of the Mytratti could tell him his ideas weren't sound. When I saw what he was doing to you, I knew something was wrong but I was blinded by my research.

"I stayed with the Mytratti for a few weeks after the Breach closed," he said. "They were in a panic, looking for Goode in stations around the world, trying to contact him via their network. When they found him, however, he had a new plan. I don't know what it was, but he was convinced your father, Agata, was the key. He was the one who would make it work. He sent the Mytratti to find him.

"That's when the Nayzun hid your father. They moved him from a hiding place in Prague - we were very close, by the way, when you went looking for him there - into an oubliette off the coast of Iceland."

"What do you mean?" asked Agata. She turned to Turtle, who was also staring intensely at Mr. Kincaid.

"He's in the ocean. I don't know how or where, but that's where he is. I spoke to a Nayzun, not 411..."

"2111," said Turtle.

"It might have been. He was more 'awake' than the rest, the way 411 was. He was clearly enlightened."

"So how do we find him? Where do we go?" asked Agata.

"I think 2111 will know. I was on the run. I still am. I'm going exploring. I think whatever is about to happen to the Mytro will change it entirely. I don't want to lose the opportunity to try what I want to try," said Mr. Kincaid.

"What do you want to do?" asked Agata.

"Your father was researching how Mytro stations were formed and brought into being. I was studying stations on other worlds. The problem is that you can't imagine those other worlds – there are no names for them. But we do have star charts. If I say 'the planet closest to Alpha Centauri,' I suppose I'll go there."

"Space exploration?" asked Turtle. "Are you sure you want to do this?"

"What else do I have to do on Earth? I've disgraced myself. I can't work with the Mytratti or the Guild and there's lots we need to learn about the Mytro."

"We're trying to stop the Mytro," said Turtle. "Shut it down."

"I don't blame you, at least on Earth. Our Mytro has gone mad and the people serving her are even madder."

"Who? Mr. Goode?"

"Absolutely. I also discovered their plan. It's terrible. You need to take a message to Ms. Banister. I know what he is doing. I just don't know which hangar they are using for the launch. It's something terrible, guys. Can you remember what I'm about to tell you, or do you want to write it down?"

Agata pulled out a notebook and pen.

"If we find out you're lying..." she started.

"I'm not lying. I'm sorry. I truly am. Now please, let me tell you what's going on."

Mr. Kincaid told them what he knew. The Mytratti were attempting to create a new army of Nayzun. They had decided that Nayzun were the Mytro's hands, the only way it could interact with the world. The belief, then, was that if they created their own army of Nayzun, controlled by the Mytratti, then they could take control of the tunnels. Whether this was true was unclear, but Mr. Goode was willing to try.

Mr. Kincaid didn't know how they'd create the Nayzun. He suspected they had a source of life, perhaps from off the planet.

Agata snorted when she heard this.

"That's silly," she said.

"I have no idea," said Mr. Kincaid. "No idea at all."

"So we have to stop this," said Turtle.

"If you can. I think the Conductor's Guild is strong enough to put up a fight, and there's no knowing how the Mytro itself will react. There's another wrinkle too. Somewhere out there is another being, something else that is trying to control the rails. It is a human, we think, but with a Mytro's power. We don't know where they are, but they – more than anything Goode can do – could be the answer we need to change the Mytro for good. If there is another Mytro, another controller of the rails, then the argument is over. We must make sure the Mytratti don't get ahold of him or her. That could spell a real problem for us all."

"So what are you going to do? You and Goode got us all into this mess. This was your fault," said Turtle.

"Please, Turtle, believe me. I never wanted what happened. I am a scientist, a researcher. When I met Mr. Goode, I didn't have much money, my business was going under, and I was amazed by this new world – just like you were. But I understand now what is happening, what kind of changes are taking place. This isn't ours to control any more than we can steer a storm. And this is a storm. It's gathering quickly."

"Go to the Guild. Tell them about the Oubliette. Take this letter." He handed over a sealed manila envelope addressed to Ms. Banister and then smiled and fished out his phone. He took a picture of the two of them with it and showed them.

"Why did you do that?" asked Turtle, surprised.

"So I won't forget myself again," said Mr. Kincaid. "How are Nick and Nate?"

"They hate me and they miss you," said Turtle.

"God, what have I done?" said Mr. Kincaid, near tears.

"Where is my father, Mr. Kincaid?" asked Agata.

"2111 will know. I promise. Again, I'm sorry."

Turtle and Agata walked away, leaving Mr. Kincaid at the foot of the statue. His face was so sad, so thin, so strange, that Turtle had a feeling he was telling the truth.

"I think we can trust him now," said Turtle.

Agata was angry and deep in thought.

"I said I think we can trust him now," said Turtle.

"I'll believe it when I see it," said Agata angrily just before her phone buzzed. It was a message from Ms. Banister.

Emergency meeting. Please hurry.

Agata looked up and showed Turtle. He nodded.

"Mr. Partridge said something about a meeting. Let's head over."

CHAPTER TWENTY-FIVE

Knock Knock

Mark tried the front buzzer. No answer. Then he tried the door. It opened. Someone had disabled the magnetic bar that held it closed.

"So far, so good," said Mr. Partridge.

They climbed the stairs slowly, listening all the way. Despite what he told the monk, Mr. Partridge was scared. The maps and journals showed Mr. Partridge something odd in this part of Brooklyn, some sort of custom station that had been made a decade before by a mad member of the Mytratti. He didn't want to tell Turtle anything yet because the last Breach had almost destroyed them all. It was his duty to keep Agata and Turtle safe, although he would never tell Turtle that.

Mr. Partridge carried a map and now he consulted it. Ms. Banister had given it to him early on, during the first investigations of the Breach, and it detailed the building of this station by a group of Portuguese Mytratti.

It had been hand drawn in indigo ink on the back of a brown envelope and showed that the station was inside an apartment building, on the third floor. Someone had written "Secured" in pencil and circled it, but Mr. Partridge had no clue what that meant.

They arrived on the third floor, and Mr. Partridge looked around. The first door he came to had the family's name written on a little card next to a dirty doorbell, but there was another door on that floor. It was made of metal and painted dark grey. The little card holder was empty, and four keyholes ran up and down the door. A large peephole poked out like a shiny proboscis.

It was a "secure" door, Mr. Partridge thought, looking again at the word circled on the map, and he knocked.

This had been a strange ride. Since he had started working with Mr. Llorente, he had learned so much. He had originally read mathematics at Oxford and studied physics at Stanford. Now, however, everything he had learned was completely null and void ... or was it?

Mr. Llorente had posited that the Mytro existed without the train cars, that the train cars were a human construction, necessary to convince the fragile minds of humans to roar into the dark tunnels without going mad. They both had a theory that the Mytro was some sort of wormhole, a system of connected forces that allowed for entanglement. He didn't believe that the Mytro allowed for instantaneous travel – something more like instantaneous motion.

The travel still happened, the distance cut to pieces by a strange force, but the time was reduced by whatever forces kept the Mytro in check. It was the sort of scientific puzzle that researchers far more intelligent than him would love to tackle, but he couldn't tell anyone. The resulting tumult, confusion, and fear it would generate would change the world forever, so they toiled in secret, trying to understand what the Mytro really was.

Perhaps, behind this secure door, was an answer.

Mr. Partridge knocked again.

The door remained closed, and Mr. Partridge turned around to face Mark. Could it be the wrong building? The wrong apartment?

He turned the knob, the door opened, and a little dog raced through the door and out into the hall. Mr. Partridge turned to look at it for a moment then turned back to the open door.

I beg you. Please, get help. Leave here, whispered the Nayzun through Mark, the voice buzzing in his head like a mosquito.

"I've been charged with a mission and I must complete it," said Mr. Partridge. "If there is danger here, I must let the Conductor's Guild know. There is no benefit to remaining in the dark."

Mr. Partridge saw a shabby wall fronted by a small end table. It was immediately clear that the wall was fake, and a quick look around confirmed that it was freestanding and a few dozen feet long. It was big enough to fill the door with floral patterned wallpaper but not big enough to fool anyone paying attention. Then two figures walked to the door from behind the wall.

There, gun in hand, was Mr. Adams. Next to him stood Mr. Goode.

Mr. Goode was smiling.

CHAPTER TWENTY-SIX

I Do

Ruth listened to the tunnels as she roared down them like a lion, whooping past stations, listening to the Nameless Ones as they sang in the dark.

Today was an exciting day for her. The children were moving through the tunnels. She wanted to talk to them.

But she was shy.

She built a station and stood in it, thinking.

The children were sad. She knew why. The little man had died. He was their friend.

She pulled out of the tunnels and stood over them, looking.

She asked the Nameless Ones.

Who is the girl?

That girl is my blood, said one of the Nameless Ones. *I remember her.*

Ruth nodded. *I see. And I can help her?*

You can, if you wish.

I do want to, said Ruth.

And she soared through tunnels into the dark.

CHAPTER TWENTY-SEVEN

Endgame

The room that surrounded the small, fake wall was immense. It could have held airliner after airliner with room to spare. Multiple football games could be held in the vast area, and darkness swallowed the floor farther back.

As Mr. Partridge marveled at this strange room, everything around him moved in slow motion. He looked up at the blue lights high above the fake wall and then examined the floor. This area here was tiled, but the rest was the blackest obsidian shot with tiny pinpricks of bright reflective rock.

Next to Adams and Goode stood an older man in a plaid jacket. He was grey and drawn, confused by this mess. The little dog ran back into the apartment and barked half-heartedly at them.

Mark followed Mr. Partridge inside, carrying the Nayzun with him. He looked around the space, dumbstruck.

"I suspected as much. Another Breach and another opportunity for mayhem, eh, Goode?" said Mr. Partridge. The taller man moved toward the interlopers, but Mr. Goode stopped him.

"My dear friend," said Mr. Goode. "How did you find us? And who is your companion?"

"You leave a wide trail," said Mr. Partridge. "Like a slug. The Guild has known where you were for the past few days. One of our members followed you to Brooklyn and we found a map in some old research. Ms. Banister suggested that you might be here, but she wasn't certain. This man with me also came to hunt you down. You're in demand."

"Well, excellent sleuthing, my boy. Excellent."

"You need to leave here," said Mr. Partridge. "We're going to close this place in a few hours. I've already sent for backup. The Guild has engineers to manage this sort of thing."

Mark suspected this was a lie. Mr. Goode knew it was.

"Look around you, Partridge. What do you see? Limitless space to do the things we need to do. The Mytro has given us these strange opportunities and you want to squander them. You and yours are exhausting. Everything is dangerous, not to be trifled with. You're more conservative than Thatcher."

"What are you doing here? More enslavement?"

"It's not enslavement if they come willingly. The goal is absolute freedom," said Mr. Goode. "I'm the Pied Piper and this is my mountain."

Mr. Partridge laughed.

"You and freedom, Goode. You preach it endlessly and it always ends up with someone in chains," he said.

"I'm not trying to convince you, but I will tell you a story. In the Philippines there are a series of caves called the Kabayan. They are full of amazingly preserved mummies - thousands of them. Each of those mummies were buried alive by the ignorant sods who thought they were appeasing what we now know as the Mytro. The Mytro wanted workers. Those ignorant savages had no idea what they were doing, but we do. We know how to send strong men and women to the place where Nayzuns are made. They will not suffer. They will live forever. And it's voluntary. These people agree to all our terms and they sign our contracts. They want this."

"You're offering a deal with the devil," said Mr. Partridge. "These people don't want this. If they knew the truth—"

107

"People like this don't want to know the truth. And they will be so thankful to be free of everything that ails them. Do you know who I have waiting for spots? Cancer patients, men and women waiting for transplants who will never get them, the chronically depressed. We're doing them a favor. We're saving them."

"That's as naive as it is terrible, Goode, and you know it. I won't let you do this."

"You, Mr. Partridge, won't stop me."

"Why do I need to? Humanity will not go along with your plan," said Mr. Partridge.

"You would be surprised," said Mr. Goode. "Now, the one thing I can't let you do is bother us, so come with us, Mr. Partridge. Come to the enlightened side. What do they say? We have cake."

"There's no way that can happen, Goode."

"Then you leave us no choice. You and your friend can't leave here."

Mark grabbed Mr. Partridge's arm, and he felt the Nayzun leave his body and move somewhere else.

Mr. Adams came forward, a small gun in his hand, and fired. The noise was surprisingly loud in the small station and it startled Mr. Partridge.

Then he felt the pain.

As the slow realization of what had happened passed from his brain down to his body, Mr. Partridge fell with a soft sigh. Mr. Adams pointed at Mark and pulled the trigger a second time. There was a click ... and nothing.

Run, said the ghost.

The gunman shuddered momentarily as the Nayzun took control of his body and forced him to throw the gun into the darkness. Mark turned to the door and yanked it open. He ran down the hall and then the stairs.

He heard shouting from the apartment and then felt the whistling wind pass him and move out onto the street. He pulled out his cell phone and reported a murder. The little dog, startled by the noise, stood at his feet. It must have followed him down the stairs into the cool afternoon and so he picked it up and ran.

Part II

CHAPTER TWENTY-EIGHT

Shrinking Man

Hernando Llorente's quartz watch had stopped after the space behind the crystal clouded with water. He tried to tell the time by looking at the light coming through the translucent walls, but he had forgotten the color of day and night. This place was filled with a strangely diffused murkiness all day, a glow that seemed to come from, not through, the walls. It kept him awake.

"I am Hernando Llorente," he said again, endlessly reminding himself of his own identity. He didn't want to forget it in the unceasing light.

The light was mostly uniform - sometimes brighter but often a murky grey that could mean either a moonlit night or an overcast afternoon. He assumed, though, that he was sleeping about twelve hours a day based on the sessions of darkness and light. As time passed, he felt himself weakening, so he tried to keep himself fit by pacing around the oubliette and doing push-ups and sit-ups. He still had plenty of food, but he wished someone would come and let him out.

"I am Hernando Llorente," he said again and again, like a mantra.

On this day - if it was a day - he decided to try running in place. He did it for an hour - or at least for what felt like an hour – then he stopped and did some push-ups. He wished he had more water for bathing or at least a few more containers of wet wipes that he found in one of the boxes, but he didn't seem to smell very badly. Air came through the walls somehow, and the temperature was always tepid - not cold, not warm, but acceptable. He had brought with him three T-shirts and extra underwear and socks, although he didn't see much point in changing very often. He wasn't comfortable, but he would survive.

Sometimes he talked to the shadows outside the walls, things that floated by slowly and that vibrated the room. What was he in? He looked at every inch of the room. It seemed to be made of glass blocks, but the blocks let a little water through and they were slicker than glass, almost organic. They were stacked on each other but were held together with no visible mortar, which suggested that there was some sort of vacuum holding them together.

Then he remembered: this was a Mytro station. It didn't "exist" in space, and if he were underwater, there would be no interface between the water and the wall, at least based on the theories put forth by the major Mytratti. They believed the Mytro stations did not actually take up space or interact with the substance surrounding it. Before atomic theory, the Mytratti called the stations "motes" - infinitesimally small yet having the strange characteristic of expanding into reality when viewed directly by humans (and, presumably, animals).

The question was, then, did the Mytro stations exist when the doors were closed? And were they all made by humans and designed to a human scale? He doubted that sincerely, especially since he knew the Nayzuns. Could this be an alien room? Something not made or designed by a human?

The questions circled in his head madly. He would ground himself by repeating his name, the names of his daughter and wife, and the things he was sure of: that he was alive, that he would get out, that he was safe. But these questions kept squirming, asking to be answered. Was this an alien room? Was he on Earth? Was this even a Mytro station?

Some hours the questions grew, dwarfing him. Some hours they fell back into a dull hum. He wanted to do more research, to know more about what he was going through, but he had no paper, no books, no way to record his thoughts. Some hours he found himself hyperventilating in frustration. Other hours he sat in a stupor, something so deep and saddening that he wished he was unconscious.

He now knew what it felt like to be in prison - the endless hours, the quiet, the fear, the lack of control. It was as if the room got smaller as his panic filled it, but every time he woke in the crepuscular light coming through the translucent walls the room was the same: it was still wet, and the food and water were still arrayed before him.

Then, that morning (or afternoon?) the room got smaller. He had closed his eyes for a moment, and when he opened them, everything had shifted. The food moved closer to him, as if it had scooted across the floor. A bottle of water had rolled slightly, exposing another part of its pasted-on label. The room was getting smaller.

He had not allowed himself to panic before, but now it made sense to. He closed his eyes, and for the first time since his days as an altar boy in the *Basilica de Santa Maria del Mar* ... he prayed.

CHAPTER TWENTY-NINE

Someone to Watch over Me

R uth felt everything. She saw everything.

She hadn't spoken to anyone in a while. She spoke, briefly, to a woman named Ms. Banister but she was afraid to give away too much. Now she heard the Nayzun talking to the Kincaid man about the man in the ocean. She decided to help.

She leaned in over the Mytro.

She spoke, and her voice rang in ten thousand heads. Their stalk-like necks turned towards her and listened. She asked them where the man was. There was a deep whispering.

One of us who left us placed him there. It told me, said one of the younger Nayzun.

Can you remember what he said?

The voice whispered the name of the place. It was a strange place. She leaned over to look at it.

There he was.

But that poor man. He was sick. He was hurt.

Ruth went to him.

She surprised him and he surprised her.

I'll get you out, she said.

CHAPTER THIRTY

Fire First Time

The ghost took Mark through the Mytro, searching. Inside this body, this willing body, 411 noticed, he was constrained deeply and felt as if he wore blinders. The human, Mark, was still able to communicate but didn't, probably out of sheer wonder.

Once they had left the apartment 411 found the nearest stop hidden in a secluded spot in the park a few blocks away. They entered quickly and a train arrived almost immediately, dust fluttering from old wooden beams. 411 and Mark rode through crystal stations that glinted in the light of moons that were not there. They moved through great underground hangars, dark but for the blinking eyes of the other Nayzun. He rode Mark past a pile of ash that sparkled like the stars against the dead night.

All the things 411 knew as a Nayzun were now new to this man's eyes.

Are you comfortable? asked 411.

Yes. Why do you need me? answered Mark.

To move. Each of these rooms is a soul trap. I cannot pass from one to the next. I move more slowly without a host.

Mark gulped, or at least tried to, and 411 loosened his grip to make Mark more comfortable.

They passed through station after station – big stations and stations as small as closets. They appeared inside rock, a feeling that Mark did not enjoy.

They appeared in open space for an instant and then moved back onto the rails, the impossible sound of train wheels rattling around them.

What is all this? asked Mark.

This is my home. This is where I lived for centuries. Humans aren't ready for where I'm going. I'm trying to get us closer to the center of things.

The center?

They moved farther into the deep dark and then a fire blazed around them. It was impossibly hot, impossibly angry, and it flared up in an instant, catching the breath in Adam's throat and singeing the ends of his hair.

This is the center, said 411, pulling them out of the darkness. *And it is not happy to see us.*

CHAPTER THIRTY-ONE

Spirits

*Y*ou've been crying.

Mr. Partridge lay alone on the floor in a dark place. A girl stood over him, radiant. She wore a blue dress covered in sparks.

He looked up at the girl. She was evanescent, and he could see right through her into the darkness of the Breach. She was beautiful.

"Not crying, just disappointed."

Who are you? she asked. *Are you hurt?*

"Yes, clearly there's a bit of a problem."

The girl entered Mr. Partridge, and he felt a chill as she settled into his wracked frame. She tried to soothe him.

Did these men kill you? she asked.

"They shot me, yes. Who are you?" answered Mr. Partridge, speaking to her in his own head, his voice echoing through the pain.

My name is Ruth. I live in Ohio.

"Wonderful. I believe I've heard of you, Ruth, or at least a rumor of you. You can dream things and make them real, yes? You told Ms. Banister about the pods. You've been helping us."

Yes, I think that's what I can do. I haven't really begun to understand it. There's a boy here who helps me, but I'm scared of him now.

"Interesting. Did he give you his name?"

No. I just know what he looks like. He comes to me sometimes. He's the Mytro, now.

"Very interesting. I have a request. Can you carry a message for me? I doubt I have long."

The ghost smiled inside him and Mr. Partridge felt warm.

In this place you have forever. These places are soul traps. If you want to leave, I can help you so that you avoid the Mytro. But what can I do for you?

"I need you to tell my friends what happened. It's a very curious thing, this."

There's not much they can do, I'm afraid.

"So I'm dead ... or dying? Can you tell?"

The girl looked at him. *Dead. If it's any consolation, this life is as good as any other, I've found.*

"Oh, I know," said Mr. Partridge. "But there's something to be said for a corporeal presence."

He came to realize he wasn't talking, only thinking. There was no sound where he was, in this dark hangar.

There are ways.

"I'm learning that. Until then, can you help me send the message?"

What is it?

"We need to tell the Conductor's Guild what is happening here."

The girl looked around, then looked off in the distance, concentrating.

Let's see what we can do. I'll be back.

And in an instant, she was gone.

And Mr. Partridge was completely alone.

CHAPTER THIRTY-TWO

Dark Deeds

Mr. Goode looked around the hangar. He had narrowly escaped a place like this, not long ago. When the previous Breach – a huge structure that had been built as a station to hold workers – exploded into a rage of fire, the Mytro collapsed in on him and chased him through the tunnels. He had ridden the Mytro to a dark place, far from civilization, and escaped just as the fire began licking at his heels.

When he boarded the Mytro to escape, he thought to himself, *Take me away from here*, and the Mytro obliged, cruelly hauling him from the old Breach and to a new place, someplace high and cold and strange. When the train stopped, the doors opened, and the chime dinged twice. He refused to get off. It dinged again, insistent.

Now he was back, but this Breach wouldn't be a place of failure. It was a place of correction, of repair. He would take back control, make the Mytro great again.

But first, he noted his biggest problem: Mr. Partridge, who lay before him, gone. He was beatific. Mr. Goode hated this sort of thing, this sort of trouble. Mr. Partridge had been a worthy adversary. Not worth a bullet, to be sure.

"This is quite a problem, Adams," he said. The other man grunted. "Take him into the dark. Don't make a mess."

Mr. Adams obliged.

He turned to Mr. Ioli, the guardian. This old man was going to be another problem. He had lived in the Breach for a decade, and if he wandered off and started telling people about a hangar in an old New York apartment, Mr. Goode's vision would be, to say the least, compromised.

He figured that, with a bit of help, he could turn it into something that the whole world could use and enjoy, something that would make him a little money in the process and something that wouldn't frighten the riders. He wanted to turn the Mytro into the Tube, to make it as comfortable to ride the Mytro from New York to London as it was riding the rails from Paris to Lyon. But the Mytro was a fickle, angry thing, and he need to get rid of that fickle, angry spirit, to tame it and turn it into something. Or at least appease it. That would be his first step: sacrifice.

He turned to look back at Mr. Ioli. Perhaps the best way to move forward would be to bring the old man along for the ride. He wouldn't eat much, clearly - the little fridge here was a testament to that - and whatever had to happen would happen as they traipsed through the tunnels. Perhaps he could put him in the High Castle where some of the Mytratti could look after him.

And with that thought, Mr. Goode decided: the old man wouldn't be allowed to stay and he wouldn't be held prisoner. He would just be put into a very, very inconvenient place.

They walked with Mr. Ioli to the Breach tracks and a train rolled up. The bell rang once and the doors opened.

Mr. Ioli gasped.

"Yes, my friend. All along, this was right under your nose," said Mr. Goode.

They boarded the train, and it rolled silently into the dark.

CHAPTER THIRTY-THREE

On the Lane

The Conductor's Guild met in a large home that looked out upon a secret garden. It was located at Little Ealing Lane and took up the whole house, which once belonged to a rich member of the Guild. Now it was one of those regal estates that tourists passed by, wondering who lived inside. Turtle stood in front of it, always amazed by the size.

They pressed the buzzer on the red door, and it opened onto a front foyer that looked like any other opulent British home - deep, dark wood, porcelains, hunting scenes on the wall - but this was only a small portion of the Guild Hall.

Turtle didn't know the small, old man who opened the door, but he smiled and let Turtle and Oz in.

"Mssrs. Fulton and friend, I presume," said the little old man in a soft British accent.

"Yes. Thank you."

"No, thank you, sir. For all you did."

Oz elbowed Turtle. "What did you do?" he whispered, looking around the foyer.

"Long story," said Turtle.

This house was made up of three houses attached to each other with one large front face consisting of three other façades. Inside were laboratories and workshops where members of the Conductor's Guild had performed their own experiments on the Mytro years before. Now the house was used primarily as a meeting place and a location to keep track of all the members who used the 13 app to map every nook and cranny of the network.

The Conductor's Guild aimed to be the most complete resource for Mytro riders on Earth, and their multiyear mission had been nearly complete when the Breach closed. Unfortunately, of late, the app was incomplete because things were changing so fast on the Mytro that no one could keep up. So it was decided that in the future the Conductor's Guild would act as sort of a patrol group to make sure that things remained safe and usable. Conductor's Guild members were regularly visiting the house on Little Ealing Lane and taking their patrol orders, spending a few hours a day riding between stations and ensuring that everyone was safe.

Ehioze gestured to Oz, Agata, Maya, and Turtle to sit down, then he smiled brightly and hugged Agata.

"It's just starting," he said.

Ms. Banister took to the lectern, looking ashen and frightened. She was a short woman with black hair and a white streak down the side. She looked ageless – not old, not young – and she wore a dark-purple dress and light-violet heels. Before she began running the Guild, she had been a teacher.

"Friends, it is my great sorrow to announce that our founding member, Leslie Partridge, has been killed. I've confirmed his death with a new contact of ours in Brooklyn, New York. The Nayzun have also helped us pinpoint the location of who we suspect is his killer. It was Mr. Goode, and he has found a new Breach, this one bigger than the last and more powerful," Ms. Banister continued. "I would propose a moment of silence in memory of Mr. Partridge."

"Did she just say Mr. Partridge ..." whispered Agata.

"Yes," said Turtle. He wanted to cry. His eyes were hot and the skin around his cheeks was tight and dry. Who would kill Mr. Partridge – and why?

The whole room was quiet for a moment.

Ms. Banister looked down at her lectern and then said, "According to reports, Mr. Partridge was investigating information about a large Breach in Brooklyn when he ran into a member or members of the Mytratti. When we knew it was safe, we visited the Breach and found his body. It is being taken care of by some of our kinder members. It was a horrific thing to see and a horrific thing to know that people are still mad enough to take lives over something as valueless and capricious as the Mytro.

"I ask all of you to take special care as you move through the Mytro in these next few days, and if you see anything out of the ordinary or find yourself in a situation that could be dangerous to you or other members, I ask that you simply walk away or, should I say, ride away. Nothing in the Mytro is worth dying for. It saddens me greatly to think that Mr. Partridge died to protect something that does not have our own best interest at heart.

"Many of you have noticed already that the 13 app has stopped updating and that many of the stations are now missing or have moved," she said. "The entire system is changing in ways that we cannot understand, and we are concerned that things may change to a degree that will destroy or otherwise damage many years of hard work. We believe this new Breach – actually, it was made by the Mytratti a decade ago but it is new to us - is a depot, designed to capture and ship something or someone. We aren't quite sure yet."

Ms. Banister nodded, and the lights fell. A projector began showing scenes from inside the Breach. They had captured images of Mr. Ioli's sparse bed, the fake wall, the little refrigerator. The flash could not penetrate the darkness around this little oasis of livability, and the photos looked spooky, empty.

"I also think we have something very interesting on our hands. Before Mr. Partridge died, he was able to relay a message. He said there is another

Mytro, something that exists that is rebuilding the tunnels in its own image.

"We've long known that the tunnels and the Mytro are two different things," Ms. Banister continued. "We've taken to calling the being - the thing - that runs the tunnels a Mytratus. It's like the Minotaur of old - a creature that builds a place, rules a place, and is identified by that place. We know that the Mytratus exists and controls the Mytro. But there is another, someone else. A woman, we believe. A Mytratta."

Ms. Banister paused for a moment.

"The Mytro, as we know, is a sentient thing. The shapes, the stations, the tunnels, all are controlled or *defined* by that thing. But this new Mytratta is wresting control, piece by piece, from the old Mytratus. It's like a regime change.

"What that means for us is quite interesting," she said. "You remember Mr. Goode and the Mytratti were trying to get your Keys but we thwarted them. The Keys, however, were simple playthings in comparison to the power of the Mytratta. You can think of the Keys as dog whistles to calm a raging Rottweiler. However, the Mytratta is a whole other beast, someone who can take control and remake the Mytro in her own image."

"Someone?" asked Agata from the crowd.

"Exactly. The new Mytratta is a person. She's a girl, we believe, who has been in a coma for nearly a decade. She is the one who approached Mr. Partridge before he died."

The lights went up.

"Strange things are afoot," said Ms. Banister, "and we are working to assess just what all of this means. Until then, I ask for calm, cooperation, and respect."

A murmur went up in the crowd as Ms. Banister motioned for Turtle and Agata to follow her to the side of the room.

"You two have been out and about. It's not safe," she said. Some of the scholars were now eyeing the children, wondering who the two newcomers were. As Oz and Maya stood back, Turtle thought Oz looked nervous.

"We found Mr. Kincaid," said Turtle. "He's alive."

"I see," said Ms. Banister, whom Agata and Turtle had met after the destruction of the last Breach. Mr. Partridge had introduced the children to the group, and Ms. Banister examined the Keys but told the children to hold them. They did.

"It's not safe," she said finally. "I need you to go home and stop riding the Mytro. We'll send for you when it makes sense."

Turtle nodded, but he noticed Agata's lips were pursed. She was clearly upset or impatient. Turtle squeezed her hand.

"We'll stay off the rails," he said.

Agata squeezed back.

The meeting adjourned, and the Conductor's Guild filed out of the room and into the portable door, leaving the house quietly and without much talking. As Turtle became a more important member – many of them knew about the Breach and Mr. Goode and the destruction of the Earth Station – they would stop and talk to him after meetings, but this crowd, these researchers, were now stuck in their heads. Turtle, for his part, still wanted to cry.

"It's very dangerous," said Ms. Banister. "As I said, I don't want you two out and about, especially with your friends."

"Mr. Kincaid told me where my father was, or at least where he thinks he is," said Agata. "I'm going to go find him."

"I don't want you—" started Ms. Banister.

"There is safety in numbers," said Ehioze, cutting her off. "Don't you agree, miss?" he asked. "If we all go."

126

"I can't afford another mishap. Mr. Partridge was a dear friend, a dear man," said Mrs. Banister.

"We understand, but we have to help. We have to find out what's going on," said Turtle.

Ms. Banister paused and looked at the faces of the children around her. Turtle's face was blotchy, his tears ready to flow. Agata's was impatient, angry. Their friends – Oz, Maya, and Ehioze – were full of energy.

"I want you to split up. We have two missions today. Mr. Partridge was watching a spot in London, a restaurant. He believed it was part of the Mytratti network, a place where they were taking something into the Mytro. I'd like you to see what's going on there and report back as soon as possible."

She handed Turtle a phone number she had written on a piece of paper. "This is our new contact number. The old one is compromised with the death of Mr. Partridge. Please send news there. Mr. Partridge would have been proud," she said, looking like she was about to cry.

"You girls go to Mr. Partridge's home. See what you can find," she said. "Boys, find out what Goode is doing with these pods."

She handed them a piece of paper. Agata and Turtle read it and looked at each other.

"Be on your phone. We'll meet at your house, Agata," said Turtle.

Turtle and Agata hugged Ms. Banister while Oz and Maya stood by with Ehioze, waiting. They were ready to move. They were ready to help.

#

CHAPTER THIRTY-FOUR

Cold Comfort

Mr. Goode and Mr. Ioli disembarked at a station called Castle Breach. It was written in gold letters on the far wall, high above a sight Mr. Ioli would never forget.

The Castle Breach was gigantic but still smaller than the apartment where Mr. Ioli lived. The train opened on a room full of round pods, the metal glistening under the bright work lights. Mr. Goode led Mr. Ioli past them and he touched one as he passed. They were cold and hard and empty. In the distance, stone walls were wet with water and it was cold.

"Now what?" asked Mr. Ioli.

"You'll be my guest here for a little while. Like your apartment, the train does not stop here unless you know how to call it. Therefore, you'll be out of sight and out of mind," said Mr. Goode.

"Why don't you just leave me in Brookyln? Where is this? And how do I know your buddy won't get mean with the gun again?" asked Mr. Ioli.

"I am not a violent man. I am a keeper of violent men, a collector. What happened at your apartment was spur of the moment. You did nothing wrong, but we can't have you speaking out of turn."

"I won't talk," said Mr. Ioli. "Look at how good I kept the secret all these years."

"You did quite well," said Mr. Goode, busying himself with getting one of the pods. He went to a far-off cabinet and pulled out a pair of coveralls and a blanket. In his other hand he carried some kind of self-heating soup, two cartons worth.

"If you're hungry, you eat. If you're cold, you put these on," he said.

"I don't need to be part of this," said Mr. Ioli.

"You already are," said Mr. Goode and then he walked back to the tracks and waited for the train.

"What about my dog?"

Mr. Goode turned. "Ah, yes. She ran off, didn't she? If she comes back, I'll have one of my men bring her to you."

Mr. Ioli looked at the soup. "You don't have to do this," he said.

"Sadly, I do," said Mr. Goode. "You stay comfortable, friend. We'll be back for you soon."

Mr. Goode took out a phone and made a call. a train rolled into the station and hissed to a stop.

"The old man is safe in Eagle's Rest. You can begin prepping the first dozen or so recruits, please," he said. Then he hung up and boarded, leaving Mr. Ioli completely alone.

CHAPTER THIRTY-FIVE

Numbers

Mr. Partridge's home contained a station he called Tender Lorus. It was hidden in his study behind a trap bookcase that opened into his home and had been built using a Conductor's Key not long before. Pressing a special, worn spot on the warm wood, Agata and Maya entered Mr. Partridge's little house, now cold.

Books lined the walls and floor of the study. The close smell of wood polish and pipe smoke - Mr. Partridge took a pipe after dinner, he once told her and Turtle, but he never inhaled – reminded Agata of how comfortable she had been with Mr. Partridge, but there was nothing comfortable here now.

"What are we looking for?" asked Maya.

"Locations. We know about the hangar in Brooklyn, but we don't know where they make the pods or what they do," said Agata. She sat down at Mr. Partridge's computer, an old all-in-one Macintosh with a dusty screen.

The room looked untouched since Mr. Partridge had left. A clock ticked in a far-off room, sounding hollow through the thick brick walls. Agata began going through papers on his desk, moving them into separate piles based on what she knew about Mr. Partridge's research.

He had been looking into something strange on the Mytro. According to his notes, he had found someone or something that was not only creating new stations where none existed before, they were, more interestingly, overhauling the old stations. It almost felt like a war between two beings - the Mytro and someone else.

Maya turned on an old, leather-bound radio. It had multiple dials, including one marked Short Wave.

"Music helps me think," she said as she idly thumbed through a notebook full of maps.

Instead of music, the crackling radio brought in a low hum and then a woman's voice reading a set of numbers, repeating them over and over, carefully enunciating each word. It sounded artificial, but it wasn't clear.

"What's this?" asked Maya. Agata listened and then looked down at the desk.

"My father and Mr. Partridge loved codes. And so did the Mytratti," said Agata.

"35 31 28.56. 104 34 20.2," said the voice. There was a pause and it repeated. Again and again. A small noise, like a radio squelch, followed each message. Agata recognized it as a digital message.

"We've dealt with this before," said Agata. "Those sound like coordinates. But why would they be read out like that?"

"Oh, so it's like a numbers station," said Maya. "One of those stations that repeats numbers over and over again. They say they're some kind of failsafe in case the world explodes. If the numbers stop going, missiles go off to finish the job."

"That's possible. But it's a very dumb system. If those are coordinates, they're right out in the open," said Agata.

"Maybe they want them to be found?"

Mr. Partridge had written down a series of numbers on a piece of paper with dates and then some names of places. Prague. Ottawa. New Mexico. The numbers must have changed over time because he had four other sets written down, as well as the frequency that the old radio was tuned to.

Maya touched the computer's mouse and a small black screen appeared. On it, appearing after each digital squelch, was a message. "BREACH. BREACH. BREACH." Over and over again.

"Is the computer decoding the message?" asked Agata.

Maya clicked through the program, checking out its settings. It was called "Packet Radio Reader," and there was an audio cable snaking from the back of the computer into the radio.

"Looks that way. This program listens to the audio and prints out what was transmitted. It's a weird old technology. I read about it in computer lab," she said.

"So these are important," said Agata as she showed Maya the notes. Maya took a picture with her phone. The numbers continued to repeat themselves, and the message "BREACH" appeared again and again. "It looks like the positions changed, as well. Maybe they're sending a message? Like a scavenger hunt? Jump from place to place and then get to the final place?"

"Sounds possible," said Maya. "Why do it like this, though?"

"Because Mytratti could be anywhere, even out in inaccessible places. They need a general broadcast channel, something to connect them all together. Like an Internet."

"Wild," said Maya.

They looked through the rest of the house but couldn't find much else of interest. Mr. Partridge lived alone. A set of silverware and dishes sat in the drying rack, waiting for their owner. A photograph of Mr. Partridge and Agata's father stood on a bookshelf, and there was another photograph of Agata as a little girl pointing at a train rolling by. Agata couldn't remember Mr. Partridge from her childhood, but this photo of her and her father with the little, smiling man in a bowler showed her that they had had wonderful times long ago.

All of these things, all of these books, where would they go? Agata looked at it all and began to cry, a tear massing at the inside corner of her eye and then sliding down her face.

"He was a good guy, right. You told me," said Maya as she reached out and hugged Agata.

Agata cried harder. "I miss them both," she said.

"I know. We'll get to the bottom of this," said Maya.

They turned out the lights in Mr. Partridge's home, walked through the bookcase, and boarded the train to meet the boys.

CHAPTER THIRTY-SIX

Home Again

O z, Ehioze, and Turtle were in the middle of a tunnel when the train suddenly lurched to a stop. It seemed to turn, twisting their guts into a pretzel for a moment and then releasing them as they rocketed through the dark. The gaslights on the old train guttered for a moment and then blazed brightly as the train rolled into a station called Brooklyn Sunset.

The doors opened, and before them stood a small man holding a small dog. The man, who was wearing jeans and a nice shirt and who had short, cropped hair, seemed distant for a moment, and then he snapped back to attention when the three stepped out onto the dark platform.

Hello, Turtle. I'm sorry if I diverted your trip. I brought you here using what powers I could muster.

The man spoke without speaking. They heard him in their heads.

"411?"

Yes.

The scene was strange. The dog was shivering in the man's arms, and a scent of incense hung in the air. The man put the dog down and it huddled near his feet. Oz knelt down to call it over, and it took a few tentative steps and then jumped into his arms. Oz carefully scratched the little dog behind the ears.

I am here to help you, Turtle. This man is carrying me, helping me. I will let him go once I've told you what I need you to know.

"What's happening?" asked Turtle.

You fought the Mytro once. It is time to fight it again. I'm working to free the Nayzun. All of them. The Mytro does not want to let them go, and the Goode man is trying to replace them with new converts. Ultimately, he will fail and kill hundreds of volunteers in his pods. We need to stop him.

Oz looked puzzled but Turtle's face was set, stoic.

"So that's what he's been planning. I spoke to the Guild. They're concerned he's building another Breach," said Turtle.

That is not accurate. He is going to store some sort of travel system in the Brooklyn Breach, not far from here. He will then load the pods into a train and send it into the heart of the Mytro, to a station that is forbidden to humans. He's made a deal with the Mytro. First, he will keep my kind, my people, trapped, and then he will supply hundreds of new workers. This will give the Mytratti absolute control over the entire network.

"That's incredible. And who is this?" Turtle asked, indicating the man standing in front of him.

This is a man named Mark. He has been kind enough to let me ride him so that I can act in the real world. The little dog does not like me.

"No doubt. What do we need to do?"

You need to get Agata's father, and you need to find the Builder. She is a girl. She is in a place called Ohio. She will be able to cut the Mytro out, to remove it from this planet.

"What do you mean?"

The Mytro is a being, like you or me. It exists to take control. It is a parasite. If we can replace it with a friendly being, something less parasitic, we can keep the local network safe forever. If we fail, if this Builder fails, we will lose control.

"Is this all serious?" asked Oz, looking at Mark quizzically.

"You're asking if a possessed man with a dog telling you about a secret underground railroad system is serious? What else could it be?" asked Turttle.

"All I can say is this sure beats school."

There is not much time. We need to begin very soon.

Just then a train rolled into the station, pushing a gust of warm air in front of it. Off walked Agata and Maya.

"We were just in Mr. Partridge's and the Mytro took us here," said Agata, hugging each in turn. Oz blushed.

"Agata, I think we have some good news," said Turtle.

Hello, my child, said 411 in all their heads, with a voice like a lonesome whistle on some dark plain. *It is time. I will take you to your father.*

CHAPTER THIRTY-SEVEN

Recruits

The men and women Mr. Goode had "hired" came out of the Mytro stop and their blindfolds were removed. They stood blinking in a small white room room. It was a far cry from the messy basement from whence they had come. This was a true intake station. The Mytratti had made it look futuristic, as if this were a way station for aliens. A woman in a white lab coat held a clipboard and smiled as the followers entered the room.

"Welcome, friends," the woman said. She had thick, dark glasses and black hair, and her lips were painted in bright-red lipstick. She often hugged the more confused of the newcomers as she welcomed them to the family.

Then, as the followers grew less afraid, the woman would show them to their quarters. The women had one side and the men another. There were more men than women, so they moved some of the men into the women's area.

The pods were inside of a big room with a pile of bricks at one end, decidedly dirtier than the intake station. The pods were on wheels, but the wheels were locked.

"These pods are only temporary, friends. Soon you'll be on your way. This is but a way station," the woman said, which comforted the followers. "First, however, I think we'll have something to eat."

Three tall men in white wheeled out a table groaning with food - or at least stuff that looked like food. It looked like wafers of something bread-like

and big jugs of some milky substance, and there were crackers and yogurt and a plate of grapes. Most of the men and women took the natural-looking food and drank some of the milk.

"Please," said the woman, "I would encourage you to have some of the krill wafer. It's very filling and will keep you until we reach our destination."

She held up a piece of the bread. One of the women took a piece, and then the rest of them began to eat.

It made them sleepy.

One of the women noticed an old man sitting in one of the pods.

"Are you coming with us?" she asked him.

"I don't think so," said the old man.

The woman with the clipboard clapped her hands.

The recruits felt sleepy. They would welcome a moment's rest.

The recruits followed the woman with the clipboard up and down the rows of pods. The woman with the clipboard pointed to a pod and one of the recruits climbed in. They lay down, and one of the men who delivered the food closed the pod. The window on the pod went dark and a soothing hum came from the closed pods.

The old man watched as each recruit disappeared into their egg, as the woman with the clipboard checked off the twenty names, pulled out a cell phone, and called for twenty more.

The old man - Mr. Ioli - sighed. In the old days he would have done something, but these day he didn't have any idea what to do.

CHAPTER THIRTY-EIGHT

The Calling

Agata could hardly breathe.

Before her stood a small man speaking with 411's voice. Oz was holding a small dog. Turtle looked worried, but Ehioze smiled when he saw them. Maya, for her part, was wildly confused.

Your father was trapped. I hid him but it became too dangerous to take him out. The Mytratti were after him first but then the Mytro wanted to kill him. I had the girl create a place for him.

411's voice wafted through her head like a haze. It was gentle. Familiar. It was good to hear him again.

411 had been her ancestor, the man who first found the Mytro on Earth. He had been a farmer and a hunter, and he and his brother had found the Hill of Winds, and he had ridden the Mytro into the dark where they were changed. Now he was back. He remembered his past and hated what had been done to him. And she was so happy he had found her again.

"Abuelo," said Agata, "you're here."

I am, Agata. I've finally been able to reconnect with humanity, to find myself. It takes much energy to take this form, to ride this human, and we don't have long before I must leave.

The Mytro is a parasite, a soul-catcher. It is growing weaker, but the men you fought are trying to feed it, to help it grow. Your father knows how to stop it. It's time to go to him.

Agata's heart leapt. "Where is he?"

The walls of the station changed suddenly from old brick to polished steel. The children gasped.

Ah yes. She is here.

"Who's here?" asked Agata.

The Builder. She wants to see you.

In a flash, the room was dark, and Agata and Turtle were alone together in a place they did not recognize. In front of them stood a young girl in a blue dress that shimmered with sparks. She smiled at them.

CHAPTER THIRTY-NINE

Bleak

The house called Eagle's Rest stood over the edge of the stone cliff like a sentinel forgotten after a long war. It was built at the turn of the nineteenth century to the exacting specifications of a gentleman scholar, a Mytratti named Martin Jones-Smythe who wanted to study the passage of electrical cables through the Mytro. It was his pioneering work that enabled the tracks to be lit by gas and electrical lines because, he assumed correctly, a length of wire fed down the Mytro tunnels while attached to a train car would reach the next station without breaking. How the cables and tubes stretched was anyone's guess, but it worked, and it made him a very rich man. The resulting cable network allowed for an interconnected telegraph system that sprang up in the 1920s and allowed a group of enterprising Mytratti to cause the Great Depression.

The house was built with the spoils of that speedy communication method. The Mytrograph ran from 1910 until 1932 and was ripped out during World War II for the copper. Oddly, the wire that was fed into the tunnels came out longer than the original wires, a trick of the Mytro that gave many in the group pause and was a cause for major concern. But, for a brief period, Mytratti could get messages to each other far faster than anyone else and to more places, a fact that allowed them to corner multiple world markets without letting on that they were cheating. So the builder of Eagle's Rest built homes around the world, bringing workers and materials via the Mytro and setting up in nearly empty fields far from civilization. It would be hell for most to build in these desolate places, but thanks to the Mytro, these Mytratti were able to jet into Paris or London for business meetings, Tokyo for dinner, and then back home for a nice sleep before they rode off to New York for a board meeting.

They had built a large station in a deep subbasement, just big enough to store coils of copper or, in Mr. Goode's case, a few dozen test pods. They would be able to hold far more in the Brooklyn Breach.

Now, Mr. Goode stood outside Eagle's Rest, thinking, eyeing the bones of the old house, and planning the future.

Mr. Goode's mother, Nina Goode, wasn't married to Jones-Smythe. She was a cleaning woman who fell for his charms. The Mytratti gave her Eagle's Rest as a place to live and raise their illegitimate child. Mr. Goode knew none of this as he was growing up, but later he refused to take his father's last name because, after Jones-Smythe died, he left the little family nothing with which to fend for themselves in the dark wastes of Norway.

Mr. Goode remembered long, dark winters in Eagle's Rest. He remembered waking up cold in the Winter Quarters, the half of the house left open when the snows fell. He remembered eating simple wheat cereal and cold toast because there was no money for food, and he remembered quick trips to London where his mother would beg Jones-Smythe for more money. The Mytratti had grown quiet and irritable in his old age - he was twenty years older than Nina - and seemed to have forgotten who they both were, so he ignored their pleas. They returned to Eagle's Rest, and Nina cleaned local houses even though she lived in a mansion.

But when the money was rolling in, Eagle's Rest was a place of warmth and happiness. When Jones-Smythe came to visit and work on his experiments, they would take the Mytro into a beautiful city and have a beautiful meal. Thanks to a banking network based on the Mytro, they could get money anywhere in the world in an era when sending money was impossible. They called their network the Icarus Exchange and even offered access to special friends who wanted to be able to send telegraph messages anywhere in the world. The ticket booths, which were once supposed to act as taxation stations in some of the Mytro stops, went dark after Germany fell to the Allies. By that time, the wireless had replaced most wired communication around the globe. It had been a beautiful, heady time for the Mytratti, but the war made people less interested in the Mytro.

These days were not so heady.

This house, this Eagle's Rest, was once beautiful with bright windows that flashed in the sun of the bright Norwegian summers. Now it had fallen into disrepair. Shingles had fallen from the roof, exposing bare wood and, in places, rotten planks. The upstairs windows had been carefully shuttered years before, but now the shutters tipping and some had fallen off completely. This was Mr. Goode's home now, however. He was the last of a long line of thinkers who had come to Eagle's Rest to plot and plan. And now he was back.

Except for his two assistants and a small group of employees, Mr. Goode was nearly always alone. He controlled a small trust for about thirty remaining Mytratti, all rich men who were old enough to remember the Mytro's glory days.

He had big plans. But things got messy as the plans fell into action.

Mr. Partridge had been a mess. Mr. Goode hated messes.

Now he shivered as he walked to the edge of the cliffs and looked down. His plan was almost complete. The pods were being shipped to the Brooklyn Breach. The network was awake, the Mytratti and the Guild alike.

He was an economist by training and saw the Mytro as the ultimate multiplier, a way to make everyone equal. For so long, only the rich and powerful owned the systems of transportation. Governments owned the roads. The airlines ruled the skies. But the Mytro, with a little improvement, could topple all of those. To live in a true global village where one town was seconds from the next was a dream that could come true. If he and the remaining Mytratti could make a little money along the way, then what was the harm?

But greed did not drive him. What drove him was understanding. He wanted to see what would happen when humans wrested control of the Mytro. He wondered what would happen when the Mytro left - or if it could ever leave? In the end he wanted to see humans prevail.

He, himself, wanted to prevail.

The grass here was nearly dead, and the sun was falling over the horizon into the cold lake that stretched out before the house. It would be dark soon and he'd want to go back inside, to drink a whiskey and sit by a fire and think. But he couldn't tarry. There was too much to do. He had to populate the Breach, move the humans into place, and fire his buckshot into the heart of a monster that spanned the world. Would he succeed? He did not know.

The housekeeper, Mrs. Paul, wearing a grey flannel man's coat with big pockets, came out of the house to see him. Her head was covered in a thick shawl, and she wore galoshes the likes of which Mr. Goode hadn't seen since his grandmother died, great big ones made of grey plastic.

"Evening, Mr. Goode. Should I make you a cup of something?"

"Yes, ma'am. Please make a few meals while I am home. Five should be sufficient. I have a delivery to make. My dear friend is ill, and we don't want you catching whatever he has," said Mr. Goode. "So I'll take the food to him."

"Very kind of you," she said. "And how long will you be staying?"

"That, my dear, is unclear yet. It shouldn't be long. Long enough to recharge a bit, make some plans."

The housekeeper nodded sagely. "It's good you're back, sir. It's good to have someone here to talk to, that's sure."

"It is indeed, Mrs. Paul. It is indeed," said Mr. Goode as he turned back to face the cold lake.

CHAPTER FORTY

Instant Message

Lionel sat in front of his computer while the stamper kept producing pods. He had spent most of the afternoon trying to ask his friends about the pods, posting to a secret social network that only he had access to. He even sent it to a friend at Stanford, a rocket scientist, who was as stumped as he was.

Claude was running the stamper and Pawel was napping. They were close to their quota, and soon they'd have nothing to do.

A message appeared on his computer screen.

Hello. Are you making the pods?

Lionel replied, *Yes. Who is this?*

Someone who understands what you are building. Those pods are designed to kill the people inside them. I can't explain much right now, but they are very dangerous.

The person on the other end of the conversation pasted a video into the chat room. Lionel clicked it, then looked up at Claude and Pawel.

"Guys, take a look at this," he said.

The video showed a pod in a white room. There were no humans, just robotic arms that moved the pod like it was made of paper. It was wheeled into a dark place at the end of the room. Inside the pod, someone was screaming.

"Let me out!" they howled.

The robot arm pushed the pod into the darkness and it disappeared, winking out like a magician's trick.

Lionel looked up at the pods then back down at the video. The arms were grabbing another pod from somewhere off-camera. The video stopped.

"OK, this is seriously deranged."

"Seriously," said Claude.

"Where do they deliver these pods?" asked Pawel.

"I don't know," said Lionel. "When I get here in the morning, the new ones are gone. I haven't seen anyone around since they hired me."

"So we're making murder pods?" asked Claude.

"Seems that way," said Lionel.

We looked at the video, he typed. *Who is this?*

I can't tell you. Please just stop building. I found you through your online postings. I'm sorry I can't say more.

"All we have is one video and even that doesn't show much. That could be staged," said Claude.

"Look, they hired us to make stainless-steel pods with no clear use, no questions asked. They paid us really well, mostly to shut us up. So maybe it's time we asked some questions," said Lionel.

"Yeah, maybe it is," said Pawel while running his hand along the cold steel of the pod.

CHAPTER FORTY-ONE

Mytrocite

ello, Turtle. Hello, Agata. I'm Ruth.

H "Hello. Who are you? Can you see us?" asked Agata.

I can. It's great. What's that in your hand? she asked.

Turtle looked down, surprised. "It's a cell phone. It's like a little phone you can carry around."

Very cool. I'd like to see what the world looks like now. I have only seen the inside of the tunnels.

"What do you mean?"

The room shimmered for a moment, and an image appeared on a far wall, bronze embedded in cold steel. It was an image of a small figure in a hospital bed. Machines stood next to the bed and tubes ran to the figure.

This is what I think I look like. I haven't seen myself in years.

Agata went to touch the wall. "Where are you? Who are you?"

I don't know right now. They moved me. I'm a Builder, I think. That's what the Boy tells me.

"The Boy?"

He taught me to fight the other one. There is another Builder, the one that ruled the tunnels for a long time. It is angry because you're both hurting him. And it doesn't want me to take over.

Turtle looked at the girl. "You don't look sick," he said.

This is the image I make for myself. I bet I'm pretty ugly in real life.

"I bet you're not," said Agata. "Tell us what we can do to help."

A change is coming. The Nayzun want their freedom and I can give it to them. They suffer so much. We've been working on a plan with your father. He learned the song of undoing, the words you need to say to unlock the Nayzun. The Mytro, the one you think is the train system, is going mad. I think the only way to solve this problem is to lure it out and then shut off the stations one by one. It doesn't like to be hedged in, controlled, and it will get sloppy. I've seen it get angry. It's like seeing a tantrum. Then, when it fights me, you can begin freeing the Nayzun.

"Do you talk to the Mytro?"

Not in the way I talk to you. When I see it moving, here, it looks like fire to me. The fire grows and then makes another station or it burns it out out and creates a tunnel. I tried talking to it a few times but it won't talk back. I also talk to the Boy.

"The Boy?"

There is a Spanish boy who comes to me sometimes. He shows me my power.

Turtle thought for a moment and then smiled, amazed. "411! It's Agata's grandfather. You see him as a boy?"

He's young. Very young. Very handsome, incidentally. And he looks a little like you, Ruth said to Agata.

"He's hundreds of years old. He used to be a Nayzun but we freed him," said Agata.

He never told me about that, but age is just a number. What we need to do now is get your friend into position in a central place, one of the first places. There's a place they call the Worm Hole. It's where the Mytro began. Your friend will push the Mytro from station to station into the Worm Hole, and then I can begin the process with the Nayzuns. We can get them to safety and you can close the Worm Hole.

"This is incredible," said Turtle. "I can't believe you've been here the whole time."

I've only shown myself to a few people. They are working in secret to make me powerful so that I can leave my body and live here.

"Leave your body?" asked Agata.

So I can die. It's OK. I know what you're thinking. It's not all bad. This place catches souls and makes them real. That's what's really happening in the tunnels. Your soul is being moved from place to place and your body has to follow. When you don't have a body ... well, the Mytro either gives you one like the Nameless Ones or you just float. Your friend is floating right now, actually.

"Who?" asked Turtle.

Mr. Partridge. He'll come find you soon enough. I know this is a lot to accept. Let's go get your father and see what we can do from there.

"You know where my father is?" asked Agata. "You're the one?"

I am. The Nayzun told me. They wanted to hide your father from the Mytro. The Mytro was trying to kill him, but he escaped.

"He's alive?" asked Agata.

He is. 411 will take you to him. I have to prepare some things as the hour grows late.

"Kids don't say that," said Turtle.

Ruth looked at them quizzically. *I must have been talking to the Boy too long.*

Agata and Turtle smiled and then were winked back to the place from where they had come.

CHAPTER FORTY-TWO

She Divines Water

To Oz, Ehioze, and Maya, it seemed like Turtle and Agata had been gone only an instant. When the two reappeared, the others gave a small cheer and the little dog barked.

"It's time to go to my father," said Agata firmly as she turned to face Mark.

It's too dangerous, said 411.

Agata stared at him, her arms crossed, her face a storm. "We must find him," she said. "We simply must."

Your father is safe where he is, said 411. *I said I know where he is – not that it was prudent to search for him.*

"And you knew where he was all along, all summer. We could have found him," said Agata.

No, I didn't. He hid himself and I asked him not to tell me where, to keep me separate from their brave operation. The Builder made the oubliette and told the Nayzun what he needed to survive. I protected the Nayzuns who hid them as long as I could, but I couldn't keep them alive. The Mytro destroyed them. There is a great fire blazing at its heart. I knew that I could be tortured and convinced to tell where your father was kept, so I kept that knowledge hidden from myself.

"And now you know?" asked Turtle.

I do, but I do not want us to go there. I am allowing the man I'm riding to come back for a moment. He seems hungry.

"Don't you dare leave. We are going to find my father. We are going right now," said Agata.

"Tell us, please, sir. Please," said Turtle.

Mark seemed to frown then shake his head. He moved as if asleep, but his eyes were bright and wide open.

"He is hungry?" asked Ehioze, reaching into his bag to bring out a paper sack. Mark looked around, confused.

"Eat something," said Ehioze.

Mark, the man himself, seemed to come out for a moment and looked at them, surprised. He reached down and took a bit of the muffin Ehioze offered.

Looking at the children, he said, "I feel like I've been asleep. Where are we?"

"We're nowhere, as far as I can tell. It's been about three hours since we met. You're being controlled by a Nayzun," said Turtle.

Mark nodded slowly, looking around. "How did we get here?"

"By the Mytro. It's a train system," said Agata.

Mark nodded again. He seemed to remember something about the trains, about some kind of apartment in Brooklyn, about these children. He felt slightly sore, as if he had run a few miles. He reached up to rub his neck and it felt alien to him for a moment, then the nerve endings sprung to life and he was himself again.

The memories came flooding back suddenly. The stardust. The room in the rock. The fire at the center of it all.

It was strange, but he felt that he was doing the ghost a great favor and that he would be rewarded, karmically or otherwise, depending on how all of this ended up. He wanted to will the ghost back into his body, but he knew that the ghost was very close by; it would come by itself. He didn't have to do anything.

So he finished the muffin, drank some water that Agata gave him, then sat back and smiled.

"I hope I'm being helpful," he said. "I hope this is all worth it."

"I think it will be," said Turtle.

Mark finished the muffin and looked around. There. There in the corner. The ghost.

The ghost came back into him, and he felt it press over his mind and body like a cold sheet of ice. He was gone now, taken over by the voice that sounded like trains howling in the distance.

You children must learn patience. I can take you to your father, but there are stranger things and more important things afoot that will change everything about the Mytro today and forever. We have many things to do today. Your father's rescue is just one of them.

"Then let's do them all," said Agata. "Just tell me where he is."

Reykjavik. In the water, deep in the water.

Agata looked at Turtle and Turtle shrugged. "If we have lots to do, then we need lots of help," said Turtle. "Let's go get your dad. I think it's best if you guys start hunting for the pods. Maybe you and Ehioze, Maya? And maybe we can leave the dog somewhere?"

"I'll take it back to the meeting hall, and then we'll go to the address Ms. Banister asked us to investigate," said Ehioze.

"Is that alright, Maya?" asked Agata.

"Of course," she said, smiling. She hugged Agata and gave Turtle and Oz a kiss on the cheek. "I'll see you guys soon?"

"Definitely," said Turtle, a little too quickly.

"Now, please, *abuelo*. My father," said Agata.

As you wish, said the Nayzun.

CHAPTER FORTY-THREE

Bombs Away

The Brooklyn Breach was built by the Mytratti to house German weapons as they had planned to take over New York if the Allies fell in World War II. The original Breach was connected to a door inside a warehouse in Queens, but the Portuguese Mytratti had moved it after the war was over. The building in Queens was about to be destroyed to build a mall, and so the Mytratti had replaced Mr. Ioli's door with their own portable door. The resulting apartment was supposed to be empty, but Richie the Hammer had convinced the Mytratti to hire Bernard Ioli to keep watch.

"That guy don't talk," he told the Mytratti. And Mr. Ioli never talked.

Now, however, the Brooklyn Breach had new tenants.

In the dull light of the huge space, these tenants arranged the pods in long lines. Each pod, when bolted shut, would hold one human. Over the past hour the Mytratti had moved twenty pods that were already full of humans from Eagle's Rest to this place in preparation for the final move into a tunnel constructed for a single purpose: to send these people to their death.

One of the pods contained a grandmother from Dublin. She lived alone and wanted to live to see her grandchildren. She lay in the dark pod, waiting. Three pods to the left of her was a journalist named Miguel who was investigating Goode's claims. He wanted to see how cults worked from the inside. Now, had he been awake as he sat bolted into this metal egg, he would have regretted his choice.

There was a young woman from London named Natasha who wanted her life to really start. As she sat in the pod, she was scared that this was not the way to do it, but she could not escape. She had heard the screws tighten, and no matter how hard she pushed, she couldn't move the lid. Finally, she passed out from fear and exhaustion.

Another man had taken sleeping pills and was snoring loudly in his pod. He was dreaming of thunderstorms on the edge of the Isle of Man where he spent his summers. He was paralyzed from the waist down, and he was told that this place would heal him. He had little to lose.

There were many, many more – soon to be hundreds more. Each pod contained a human, a story. Each pod contained someone's dreams and hopes.

All the people in the pods had names. All were promised eternal life and amazing experiences. They had no idea what was going to happen.

Mr. Goode stood over them. Holding an old book in his hands, he flipped the pages idly, ignoring them as they crumbled to dust under his thick fingers. Two Mytratti he could trust stood next to him, but he barely noticed them.

"Can they hear me in those?" he asked.

One Mytratti turned to the other and shrugged. "Presumably, sir, as there are air slits."

The volunteers had come in during the day, one at a time, and entered the pods which were not sealed until the last moment. Mr. Goode did not want to disquiet the claustrophobic. Now, however, he had all the time in the world.

"Dear friends," he shouted. "I'm about to join you in a pod, but before we embark on this journey, I want to tell you how proud I am. For humans to try something like this – something so magical, so amazing – without question is a testament to the beauty of an idea, the idea that we can transcend this mortal coil and move further, deeper into the strange realm of the unknown. You will not be harmed. You will not hurt. These pods are here to protect your body as you enter the realm of the soul. We have tested this technique again and again, and we are sure it works.

"Why am I doing this?" Mr. Goode continued. "Why am I going with you? Because when we do this, when we make the ultimate change, we will become resplendent, and I want to be there when it happens. So friends, please prepare. You will be moved by loader into place, and the rest, as they say, is history.

"Thank you, friends, and Godspeed."

Some of the people in the pods clapped. The sound was hollow, like someone kicking a tin can. Then they stopped.

"Alright, lads. Let's start pushing these things onto the tracks and see what happens," said Mr. Goode quietly.

CHAPTER FORTY-FOUR

Conscience

Claude was in his small apartment in Sunset Park, drinking a seltzer and watching a crime program on TV, when his computer dinged. He fired up his mail program to see who it was.

I understand that you have access to video evidence of a massive production process taking place by the waterfront. We need your help.

Who is this? Claude answered.

Someone with answers, came the return email.

Claude typed out the whole story - the payments, the number of pods made, the size. They emailed back and forth for another few minutes.

And you have no idea where they send them?

I don't know, but it has to be huge, wrote Claude.

Thank you, wrote the strange correspondent whose email address was guild@13.co. He looked up 13.co and found a landing page, an image of the number 13 looking like an M on its side.

I'm sending some people to visit you. Will that be alright?

Claude paused, looking at the email. Should he give up the money? It was a lucrative gig, something that suited him and his team exactly. He would have to leave the country immediately. The man who had hired them, Mr. Goode, was not a kind man. Claude knew that much.

But he had to do something ... the video ... the people that would be put into those pods and sent wherever.

He emailed back with his address.

Come quickly, he wrote. *I'm waiting.*

CHAPTER FORTY-SIX

The Fire Next Time

The Nayzun led them to the station, a station with no name, where Turtle, Oz, Mark, and Agata disembarked, and then the train wheeled off with a rattle. The station was made of volcanic stone set with round jewels of what looked like red glass. The entire station - much larger than they had expected - could fit four cars and had a small iron door with a three-pointed trident shape carved deep into the metal. The floor was the color of ash but solid, made of the strange, spongy material that Turtle recognized from the floor of the Nayzun hangar.

"So if a station doesn't have a name ..." said Turtle.

Then the traveler must simply know, said 411. *That's the first obstacle.*

They tried the door, and it swung open easily as a gust of wind rushed in and a heavier gust came from behind them. They popped out onto a grassy median next to a small roadway bordered by heavy, moss-covered rocks and the flat of a deep bay.

"Where are we," asked Agata.

Turtle looked around.

"Reykjavik. Iceland," he said. He recognized the opera house, a strange square studded with colorful plates late schales. Reykjavik was nothing like Turtle expected. The hillock was topped by a glass box that looked like an elevator, and all the buildings that they saw were about five stories tall and white or tan.

This was a city of small roads, small buildings, and a wet cold that made him wish he had brought his winter jacket, but Agata and Mark were in even worse shape. Agata wore a light windbreaker, something turquoise she had pulled out of her backpack on the Mytro, while Mark wore his T-shirt and jeans. He didn't notice the cold, however, because 411 - the ghost - was still riding him. Oz took off his jacket and offered it to Agata, who waved it away. She put it on him.

"You need it more than me," he said, so she took it.

They came up in a completely empty area. They saw a long road in front of them, but no cars.

Forward, said 411.

They walked down the shore a few yards and came to a statue that looked like a skinny, silver-white Viking boat made of steel, burnished and buffed to resemble driftwood. Across the bay, dark mountains rose from the sea and stopped the scudding clouds that broke up as they hit the peaks. Even though it was late, here it was still nearly bright as day, and the sky was a blue-silver that made Turtle tired. The road along the sea was lit by sodium lamps burning bright-white in the wet.

"The only way forward is the sea," said Agata.

Mark turned his head left and right, slowly, as if just waking up and making sense of his surroundings.

I am sorry. I do not see what you see, he said. *The way forward is through the water. Your father is a few yards out. The oubliette is there.*

"Can't we just take the Mytro? Do we have to go into the water?" asked Turtle, eyeing the dark sea. He could swim, sure, but had he ever swum in cold northern waters? The coldest he had ever felt was a polar-bear dip he had taken in the Atlantic one winter during a Boy Scout trip.

Agata looked at the water differently. "Where?" she asked, then she looked at Turtle. "You don't have to go in. You can stay here. Help us when we come back out."

"You're not going in there alone," said Turtle. "End of story."

"Turtle, you can't go. I can't let you get hurt."

Turtle stood looking at the sea and then back at his friend. "I'm going to get some blankets," he said. "Don't go in until I get back."

"I won't promise," said Agata.

"Please. Don't go in without me."

"I'll watch her," said Oz.

We must leave this place, said 411 suddenly.

"Why?"

The Mytro. It knows we are here. It's coming.

Mark's eyes turned crazily in his head, like a frightened horse. It chilled Turtle to see the fear there and the strange control 411 had over the man.

The fire is coming.

Turtle felt it before he saw it – a heat, some sort of burning sensation that radiated from the ground and through the soles of his sneakers. He had once heard of a place in Pennsylvania called Centralia that had been a mining community. Decades before, the mine had caught fire and slowly and relentlessly consumed itself, the ground itself becoming too hot to touch. Families left the town to the fire as their deep root cellars turned hot as ovens and workbenches and old clothes burst into flame. The roads buckled and trees caught fire randomly, as if someone had sent bolts from above and hit pines and maples out of spite. The town was abandoned and the fire still burned.

That's what he felt now, the heat and the power of something underground.

Agata felt it too and knelt down to touch the concrete.

Fire was coming.

First, it came out of the hillock, behind the hidden door, then it rose from a dozen different places all along the shore. It was a strange fire that burned brightly and seemed to seep from between the boughs of the hedge and along the ground. Where it touched, it burned, like lava, but it was gaseous, bubbling up and filling space that it could claw out of the dark volcanic rock of the shore. The hedge burned completely, turning into ash that rolled into the fire and was gone. And the fire was coming towards them.

The wind picked up in a gale, sea spray and rain rolling over them as the ground began to burn. The rain hissed on the melting sidewalk.

We must go, said 411.

Although the fire moved slowly, it was gaining speed, and they were backed against the sea wall. It rolled around the Viking boat's base, charring it and leaving a sharp line of ash. It was going for the water.

Behind him, Turtle heard a splash. Oz's windbreaker was on the ground and Agata was gone. Mark turned to look, turning slowly like in a dream, and then took Turtle's arm.

"Agata!" yelled Turtle. But she was gone. Oz howled when he realized where she had gone. She had gone to the water.

This way.

They ran, and this time 411 let Mark lead the way.

CHAPTER FORTY-SEVEN

Bubbles

The water was cold as ice, a cold that bit at her and tried to pull her down. Agata gasped and then took a deep breath of air. She had taken off her windbreaker in hopes of reducing drag, but her shirt and jeans were waterlogged, making it feel like she was cutting through porridge. 411 had said the oubliette was visible if you knew what you were looking for. What was she looking for?

She was about ten meters from shore now, far from the large rocks that lined the shoreline. She could see well enough in the half light. The water was salty but still teeming with life. Vegetation had kept her from moving very fast away from the rocks, but it let up a little farther out. Finally, she was in the ocean proper, with the vast dark unfolding below her.

She looked back at the figures on the shore. First, it was just Mark and Turtle, but then they were joined by a group of people who had approached the two tiny figures and were now scanning the water. A shiver ran through her as she realized how far away from shore she was swimming. It would take minutes to return, and she didn't know how much longer she could take the cold.

But she had to stand the cold. Her father was there, hidden.

She lifted her head high into the cold air, took a deep breath, and went back down. It took a moment for her eyes to become accustomed to the murk. The sky was still bright, and some of the crepuscular midnight sun broke through into the water. She looked around and could see nothing but a little vegetation and a school of small fish that roiled left and right in front of her and then skidded around her. They were agitated, moving into the darkness deeper into the ocean.

She had swum in the ocean before, along the beach in Barcelona where the water was warm and jellyfish washed up in angry tangles. It was a good kind of swimming, warm and pleasant, a welcome respite from the summer heat. This was something else entirely, a kind of survival swimming that brought to mind folk tales of mermaids and sea dragons.

Then she felt something strange. The water was warming up rapidly. Waves of heat were rushing by, brushing her legs with the sheer magnitude of the current. She rose back up and saw, behind her, the retaining wall and the shoreline shining like fire. Fire. Fire boiling the water.

She swam as fast as she could, putting her head under when she could stand it. She wished she had taken off her jeans and her socks so that she could swim more freely. It felt like she was in a jacuzzi, a current of hot mixing with the icy cold. At least, she decided, she wouldn't freeze.

She swam farther. Below her, the heat must have caught a school of fish because a dozen, then two dozen silver sprats suddenly bobbed to the surface, cooked by the current. Agata dove into the hot water and looked around.

Then she saw it, or rather, she felt it.

There, beyond the floating fish, was a dim light. It seemed to flicker in and out of existence, a will-o-the-wisp under water. She swam towards it. The water was truly hot now, close to being painful. She hoped she didn't have to swim much longer.

There it was again: the light. She dove towards it, her legs kicking madly so that she could dive through the water. She wanted to turn around to see what was happening at the shore but she didn't dare. She swam farther and deeper and kept pulling herself down through the water towards the light, her chest nearly bursting.

The light seemed to hop, moving here and there as she swam. First, it was to her left, a few meters off, then two meters ahead. She stopped, treading water, as she looked for it again. It was about three feet square and surprisingly angular – a room in the water. It moved again and then stopped in one place. She changed course.

There it was. Dead ahead.

She dove farther, deeper, and the little light was now surprisingly close.

She reached for it, her fingers probing. She would have to rise for air soon. Her lips were in pain and her lungs on fire. She decided to breathe out, just a little, into the heat, and the little water that passed into her mouth felt like fire. What was happening? Small bubbles rose from her lips to the surface.

That's how you know which way is up to escape, she thought, hoping she wouldn't be forced to remember that.

The light was now in front of her, and she touched it. It was solid, strangely so, and spongy. She reached out to grasp it, blinked, and then poked it again.

Suddenly the light grew in shape and size, exploding into something that engulfed her completely, dragging her through a membrane that felt at once solid and liquid. Bubbles rose around her as the shape began to take up space and gain form. It wasn't a square but instead a sort of ovoid with something square inside it, where the light shone. She was reminded of jellyfish on the shore, their clear bodies like water, their tentacles indistinguishable from the rivulets after an ocean wave. She almost expected it to sting but it didn't.

It pulled her. Her hand first, then her arm. Her shoulder next and her neck and then her face popped into the open space inside. Less than a second later she was inside, sprawled on the floor, facedown against hard, translucent blocks that looked like they were made of glass.

Gasping for air and blinking rapidly, she cleared the hair from her face and stood. There, a moment away from her, across the room, standing by a stack of empty boxes, was her father. He looked at her then up at the ceiling of the strange room, his mouth open in exultation.

Bubbles float up, she thought. *So does joy.*

CHAPTER FORTY-EIGHT

Blankets

Turtle rushed down the shore. Someone must have pulled a fire alarm on the top of the hill because a group of men rushed down and he heard distant sirens, the odd *wee-woo* sirens of Europe. He watched the water, scanning the dark surface that was now under-lit with peach-colored fire.

The first men who arrived just watched the strange sight. One of them took out a small cell phone and said something in a language Turtle didn't understand. They looked at Turtle and one of them spoke to him in Icelandic.

"I'm American. I don't understand," said Turtle.

"Sorry. What is happening?" said the man in softly accented English.

"I don't know. It looks like a fire. Under the water. My friend is under there. We need to get her out."

"Was there an oil fire? An oil rupture?" asked the man on the phone.

"I don't know. We didn't touch anything. Does anyone have a boat?"

The men were joined by two more men in suits and a woman. One of them, an Indian man in a handsome wool suit, gaped at the fire and then looked to Turtle. Someone explained the situation, and he and the woman spoke quickly together in Icelandic.

"Please. My friend is down there," cried Turtle. "She fell in."

The fire was now lighting up the water from below, casting a glow on the rocks around the shore. One of the men asked Turtle where she was. He pointed out to where she could have jumped in, and he pulled out a bright flashlight and scanned the water. Nothing, just something that looked like a black buoy bobbing in the cold water.

"I can't go in there until we know what is happening," asked the man. "These are deep waters."

Another man approached, concerned.

"I'm Bala. My friend has a boat. If you show me where to go, we can go look for her," he said. Water was beading on his nice jacket, and his eyes were clear and friendly.

"She swam out there because she thought someone was out there. I guess it was the bubbles from the fire. I'll go under and look."

"There's no way you're going into there. What your friend did was very dangerous. How long has she been under water?"

"A few minutes. I saw her come up," said Oz.

"Is she a good swimmer?" Bala asked.

Turtle honestly didn't know. He had never seen her swim, even though she lived near the sea.

"I think so. She should know how at least," said Turtle.

"Is she going to be OK?" asked Oz.

Turtle looked at his friend. He didn't know.

"These guys swim like dolphins," said Bala, motioning to the men gathered along the shore. "But that water is awful. Cold. And with this fire, who knows what's going on. Come with me."

Turtle followed Bala down the path towards the opera house. Beyond it was a harbor with hundreds of boats at anchor and two little lighthouses blinking in the night.

Mark remained rooted where he stood. Turtle tried to pull him away from the scene, but Mark wouldn't move. Was it the Nayzun, afraid of outsiders? Was it some strange reaction?

"Stay here, Mark," said Turtle. Mark did not move, but Turtle pretended he did and continued to follow Bala down the shore.

"What's wrong with him?" asked Bala, motioning to Mark who was now standing like a sentinel over the spot where Agata had jumped.

"He might be in shock. I think he'll be OK. We might need some blankets," said Turtle.

"There is always an aid kit on these boats and I'm sure there will be a few thermal blankets," said Bala. They were running down, his coat open and flying behind him like a tail.

Bala, Oz, and Turtle ran down the walkway to a small slip where a dozen boats were tied up. Bala jumped over a small metal gate and went to a large boat called the *Bjössi Sör*. It was wooden, painted white, with a small cabin and benches all down the side. White life preservers hung strung along either edge. Bala untied the ropes from the dock and ran to the back to start the engine. It roared to life with a belch of white smoke that rolled into the black smoke coming off the water.

"The Icelanders don't know what to make of this. Was there a spill? Some kind of oil?" Bala asked Turtle.

Turtle shook his head. "I don't know," he said. "Honestly. She saw someone in the water. We have to bring her back up and find out. I hope no one drowned."

"Point where she went down," said Bala.

By now the entire coast was lit yellow. It looked like sunrise, and the strange Viking ship, all long arms and protrusions, was silhouetted in the flame. The fire department roared to the shore and began taking stock. No one knew what to do. The water was on fire.

"We need to be quick. Grab one of the life jackets and have it ready!" yelled Bala as he gunned the engine and backed out of the slip. He was careful pulling out but then increased speed as he straightened out. Turtle pointed towards the point where he last saw Agata. Either Agata was there, in some kind of underwater station, or she was drowning. Either way, Turtle wanted them to hurry.

"Please, please. She's a good swimmer but not that good," said Turtle as a school of dead fish floated by, catching the light like silver confetti and surrounding the boat.

Bala looked down at the fish, worried, but straightened up. "Don't worry, friend. We'll get her," he said.

Ten minutes later, Agata and someone else appeared on the surface of the water. Oz pulled Agata up and hugged her. She kissed him on the mouth and Oz drew back in shock.

"Oh, sorry," said Agata, a blush rising in her pale cheeks. "I was glad to see you."

She hugged Turtle and then turned to help another figure into the boat – her father. Turtle recognized him from photos.

"All this time," Mr. Llorente kept saying. "All this time and I could have just swum out."

"Are you alright, sir?" asked Bala.

"Yes, yes. I am." He turned to Turtle, shivering, and said, "I heard just a little about you. Thank you for helping my daughter."

The fire was still raging as they motored to shore. Bala pulled out a set of blankets and handed them to Agata and her father. It took minutes for them to warm up.

"What happened?" asked Agata's father.

"The Mytro. It's changing," Turtle said. "It's bad."

"I see that," said Mr. Llorente. He hugged his daughter closely and watched the shore, fire reflecting in his fogged glasses.

Part III

CHAPTER FORTY-NINE

Crashing Down

The first pods to enter the darkness surrounding the tracks seemed to disappear, the emptiness lapping up the steel and swallowing it like some secret animal. Inside the first pod a young man named Nelson Watkins, age twenty-one, lay half-asleep, half-awake, a panic rising in him as the pod bumped and slid into something he could not see.

In books he had read about coping, in interviews with people who had tried to commit suicide – people in the depths of so much pain and anguish that they would take their own lives – they described a moment, just as they tipped over the edge (or even while they fell), when they would quickly realize that big problems were small and small problems were infinitesimal. That there was no reason to do it, no reason to tip over to the abyss.

He was in that place now, in that instant before the after. And it was terrifying.

The pod seemed to move of its own accord. It went faster and faster, a sound like wind buffeting the contours, finding the sharp parts and hitting turbulence. He wanted out and he fought to wake his body. His mind was racing, but his hands felt like they were in some kind of pudding.

Then came the pain.

Inch by inch it rose on his body, like dipping into a hot pool. He couldn't see anything, but he could feel it. He felt he was burning, being cut, slice by slice. Each nerve touched something electric and he finally woke and howled.

Then it stopped.

What are you doing? It was a girl's voice. Quiet, caring.

"I'm dying," he said.

No, you're not. Just reach out.

He reached out. The pod was gone. He was in absolute, total darkness. It swam around him, and he felt things moving in it.

"I can't see."

A light sprang up, far away, like a candle in a window.

"Where do I go?"

I need you to stay here for now. There are more of you. Focus on that light. Don't try to move toward it. Just stay where you are.

"Where am I?"

You were about to leave the planet. I stopped you. There are more coming.

"They told us we'd gain eternal life," he said.

Why would you want that?

Nelson didn't know.

You're going to be fine. Just sit still. I can't round you all up if you keep moving.

"I'm not moving," said Nelson. "What about the old man?"

Old man?

"He didn't look happy. He was where the pods were."

I can go get him. You stay here. Just sit still. I'll get you out of here in a few minutes.

"Thank you," said Nelson.

You're welcome.

And in a blink, the voice and the girl were gone. The light, the will-o-the-wisp, glinted in the distance, a warm reminder that he was still alive.

CHAPTER FIFTY

Padre

"*Agata, mia amorcita,*" said Mr. Llorente, holding his daughter close, his hands on her back, his familiar smell enveloping her. She hadn't seen him in over a year, and the exhaustion and fear and anger that built up over that period flowed out of her. She wanted to hug her daddy, to cry out, to fall to her knees, but he held her up.

They were in a cafe not far from the water. It was the only place open where they could get warm. The officials - the Reykjavik Police and Fire Departments - seemed to forget them in the tumult at the docks. Many of the boats there were burning, and the strange opera house by the water was lit by red fire.

Mark sat at a table, dozing. The ghost let him go and he immediately crumpled, as if the air had been let out of him. Oz was very nearly asleep as well. They all looked exhausted. Oz had gotten wet during the fire and now he shivered with cold. He drank a hot chocolate.

"*Agata, mi amor,*" Mr. Llorente whispered, "how is your mother?"

"Fine," said Agata. "She's with the Guild. She'll be happy to see you."

"First, we have to finish this business," he said. "Tell me, how did you find me?"

Turtle sipped tea and eyed a package of licorice he had never seen before. "The Nayzun," he said.

"A 2111 and *abuelo*, 411, led me to you," said Agata. "2111 said it was too dangerous but we had looked for a year. We never gave up."

"I know about much of this. *Abuelo*?"

"411. He is a Llorente, from long ago. He was the first human Nayzun, the first one converted from human."

"This is amazing. That's what Mr. Partridge and I have been trying to understand – how the Mytro creates Nayzun."

"That's another thing," said Agata, looking down, holding back tears. "Mr. Partridge is dead,"

Turtle looked up at Mr. Llorente.

"It's not true," said Mr. Llorente.

"I'm afraid it is. We didn't see him, but it's true," said Turtle. He told Mr. Llorente about the meeting at the Guild. Mr. Llorente slammed a palm on the table, jarring the girl behind the counter.

"This is too much, too much," said Mr. Llorente. "This has gotten too far out of hand. This was once an academic exercise, a lark. Goode and his men have turned it into murder. We have to get out of here," he said. "You boys should take Mark back. I'll go back to the Guild with Agata."

"With all respect, sir, we'd prefer to keep going," said Turtle. "We've been tasked with visiting a place in London. It sounds like it's where Mr. Goode is sourcing his Nayzun. And there's another place, in Brooklyn, where they're building the changing pods."

"I'll go to London with my father," said Agata.

"I'll go to Brooklyn. Mark, Oz, you guys can go home. Oz, do you know how to get Mark back to his place?"

"I'm staying with you guys," said Oz. "This is our mission. We're here to help."

"We can't ask you to do that," said Turtle.

"Save the martyr routine, buddy. This is amazing," said Oz. "I'm in."

"Me too," said Mark. "I've come too far. I'll wake up."

He smacked himself to bring a little blood to his cheeks, and Oz stood up and stretched.

"So we all go and do our part," said Agata. "But we all have to be very, very careful."

The nearest station was unsafe after the fire, so they had to go deeper into the city. It was still light out, in the early evening, and cars and people passed by on their way home from work. Turtle, Agata, and the rest of the band looked like weary travelers caught in a long layover.

The next-closest Mytro stop was inside a youth hostel and brewery. It was next to a bathroom, inside a broom closet, so each one of them approached the bathroom one by one and then met up in the small station, waiting for the train. A sign above the tracks said Kex Station.

"So we split up," said Turtle. "Where do we meet?"

"Where did Partridge die?" asked Mr. Llorente.

"Brooklyn ... I think," said Turtle.

"Then we meet there. One hour. Do what we can and regroup."

Agata and Turtle hugged. The train came, and they all boarded, Turtle asking to go to Brooklyn and Agata asking to go to London. A moment later they were there.

CHAPTER FIFTY-ONE

Lost and Found

Things were going badly. Mr. Goode could tell.

They had transferred the first few full pods from Eagle's Rest and the ones he threw onto the tracks were gone but nothing happened. It was like they disappeared. And he had hundreds more podcs arriving. This was to be their staging station, but nothing was working.

Mr. Goode stood in the Brooklyn Breach, listening for the differences in the air, sniffing for ozone and dust and darkness that had long gone undisturbed.

His men were in the workshop stop, among the pods that had already been built, preparing to move them over to the Breach. It would take time, and they would move only a few at a time. The Mytro had been cooperating, but now something was wrong.

Now the Mytro was disturbed.

His two men, Adams and Watson, stood next to him.

"Why are we using this spot?" asked Adams. "Why not just leave them in London?"

"This is where the Nayzun we make will live," said Mr. Goode. "It's the only place big enough to hold these pods. The captives are on their way. From England."

"They were to be volunteers," said the other man, Mr. Adams.

"They still are," said Mr. Goode, distracted. "Wrong phrasing."

Mr. Adams had a sour face. He didn't like the sound of it.

"You see, anyone who wants to join us can join us," said Mr. Goode. "We can be as convincing as we like, but all men crave what we offer. There are rules to the Mytro, rules that require certain sacrifices be made."

"So how many do we need?" asked Watson. Mr. Adams nudged him.

"I'd expect about 10,000," said Mr. Goode. "We need to understand where the pods go and if we can reuse them. They only need to survive long enough for the humans to get beyond Earth's gravity. Then the Mytro does what it must."

"But isn't that a bit bad?" asked Mr. Adams. "Are we the baddies?"

"Sacrifice, lads," said Mr. Goode. "Early man understood these rules, and they tried, desperately, to appease what they saw as a dark god. But what the Mytro really wants is workers, and if you give it enough workers, you gain control without those silly Keys. It's a shortcut no one has tried. People aren't trusting when you say, 'Go into this dark tunnel and you'll live forever.' The pods gave them a bit of drama – and it makes the trip far more pleasant. Who doesn't want to join something bigger than themselves? We are making a new Mytro, designed for ourselves, for humans, and we need humans to run it. And we need thousands of volunteers and we're getting them. They're coming to us. They're preparing for the next step."

The two were quiet as they stared into the far distance, the dark corners of the hangar. They avoided the place where Mr. Partridge had been shot.

Mr. Watson looked over at Mr. Adams, who made a slashing gesture. Mr. Goode burned with a strange fire, as if he were smoldering on the inside, and a smile rose to his lips as he imagined an army of pods arrayed like tools of war from the edge of this massive room into the far, far distance. His will would be done.

A text arrived on his phone. The children were coming.

CHAPTER FIFTY-TWO

Brother Alvaro

The posters lined Brick Lane, bold letters claiming that participants in a new program about spirituality were welcome to try out in the basement of a curry shop called Bombay Bombay. Ehioze spotted the first sign and then led Agata, Mr. Llorente, and Maya to the place.

"I've eaten here," Ehioze said, "with my mother."

The Maya and Ehioze entered the curry shop and looked around. It smelled delicious. The restaurant was staffed by a bored-looking man wearing a uniform: white shirt, black pants, red apron.

"We are here for the meeting?" said Maya, her statement half a question.

"Basement," he said, cocking a thumb to a door next to the bathrooms.

"And when you're down there, please tell those people they better order something because they are scaring away regular customers," said another waiter in a crisp London accent as he came out of the kitchen. Someone else, another waiter, was folding napkins at an empty table; it appeared to be a typical restaurant before a dinner rush.

The pair went downstairs, past a sign that led to the loos ("That's the bathrooms," said Ehioze), and into a large dining room that smelled like it was empty most of the year, a basement smell that Maya didn't like. Somewhere nearby a train rumbled. They were close to a Mytro stop.

On the door was a sign that read "The Journey" and another that read "Quiet Please."

Under the sign was a paragraph of text:

Our founder, Brother Alvaro (May He Be Forever in The Journey), wrote that to desire endless life was not a jealous or selfish act but the culmination of all enlightenment. Join us on The Journey as we follow in his footsteps and create the next generation of seekers.

"That's ominous," said Maya, but Ehioze shrugged. None of this made any sense.

Past the door, the waiting room was almost full, with men and women standing against the wall. They looked normal - a bit paler than most and dressed in more black - and they looked to the four expectantly. Some sat on chairs or benches arrayed randomly in the room. Others stood, reading from small books.

Two men sat at a card table as a line of quiet people signed forms with borrowed pens. Maya and Ehioze got in line.

"How old are you?" said the man.

"Old enough," said Ehioze.

"We're looking for a older crowd, just so you know," said the man as he handed over the form. "I don't want you to have to wait for nothing."

"That's quite all right," said Maya.

Ehioze noticed that something that looked like a portable door was behind the desk, leaning against the wall. These doors, created by powerful Mytratti, allowed you to put a Mytro station anywhere. If they opened the door, they could have walked through and onto a train platform. Perhaps that was the plan? To lure these people onto the platform and into the Breach?

Ehioze brought the form back to them. It was a contract, one describing something called The Journey.

The Journey is a group of like-minded individuals who hope to live forever and tell others about it on television. This is partly an acting position, but it is also a spiritual movement. By signing this contract, you agree not to reveal the techniques you will learn in the various workshops and seminars. These seminars are free, but if you join us in The Journey, understand that you may be chosen to become a full member and accept what that entails.

There was more detail, including the length of the classes (indefinite) and the cost (they repeated multiple times that the entire thing was free). Then Maya read about the pods.

Members of The Journey will experience a period in a sensory-deprivation pod. This is the first Test for partakers of The Journey.

"Eternal life?" asked Ehioze.

"What does that mean?" asked Maya.

"Not sure," said Ehioze. "This Brother Alvaro man is dead, though. He's the founder of the Mytratti. He died a century ago."

"Look," said the man. "You lot aren't going to lounge about here. There's serious work going on."

"We were sent," said Maya, "by the Mytratti."

The man behind the table stood and stared. "You two?"

Maya nodded.

"Well, tell those bunkum artists they haven't paid me yet," said the man in a whisper. "I'm a casting agent, not a cult leader. These people are going to get wise soon enough, and most of these folks are mad as birds. I'd like to have my lunch as well."

"We'll help," said Maya. "Go ahead and eat."

"Fine. Make sure everyone here has filled out the paper and then send them through the door. There's a pod waiting for each of them. Most of them are primed. If it's not primed, you know what to do?"

"Yes," Ehioze lied.

"Good. I'm going up for a slash. Get their papers, take a picture of their ID, and lead them in one at a time. We've done fifty this morning. They want fifty more by tomorrow, then two hundred a day once we figure out all these tricks."

The casting agent stood up, brushed off his pants, and climbed the stairs to the upstairs restaurant.

Ehioze looked at Maya and climbed up the stairs to lock the door.

"May, get ready. This is going to get weird," said Ehioze quietly. Then he shouted, "Alright, people, we're going through this door and we're getting away from here."

"Single file. Stand up please," said Maya, following his lead.

"What about the program?" asked a skinny woman with dreadlocks.

"We're going to be putting on a very exciting show," said Ehioze.

CHAPTER FIFTY-THREE

Back in Brooklyn

Turtle, Oz, and Mark got off at the Sunset Park stop, the last stop Mr. Partridge had visited. Mark, who was now groggy but growing more alert, looked up at the sign above the tracks and seemed to sigh in disbelief.

"What happened today?" he asked.

"What do you remember?" asked Turtle.

"Not much. I was in the temple then I was in Iceland and now I'm back in Brooklyn?"

As Turtle gave him a quick rundown of the day, Mark rubbed his shoulders and smoothed down his wrinkled shirt. They all looked like they had just run a marathon. Turtle and Oz's school uniforms were disheveled and stained and still salty from the sea water. Mark looked like he had just woken up.

"Was I helpful?" asked Mark.

"Very," said Turtle. "411 wouldn't have been able to talk to us without you. You have a special gift."

"A gift for being a puppet," said Mark as Oz helped him through the door and into an alley between two apartments, shaded from view. A few feet away, a river of cars rolled down Sixth Avenue.

"It's more like a gift of being open and kind," said Turtle. "That's important. ... OK, so we're back home, but we have a few more stops. You don't have to come."

"It's OK," said Mark. "I'm starting to like this."

Oz nodded. "It's fun, right?" he said.

Turtle's phone beeped. They had a new address from Ms. Banister.

"That's a few blocks from here," said Mark. "We can definitely walk it."

The night was warm. It was good to get back to familiar territory and they walked quickly, ignoring the bodegas and restaurants along the way, although they were all hungry. They passed a little pastry shop and Oz sniffed deeply, taking in the scent of bread.

"The last thing I ate was a bun in London," said Turtle.

"When we're done with this, we're getting chicken sandwiches," said Oz.

"Definitely."

They came to the address and rang the buzzer. A moment later a voice came over the intercom.

"Who is it?" asked the voice.

"It's us. We're with the woman you contacted," said Turtle.

"About the pods?" said the voice.

Turtle paused, confused.

"Yes?" said Turtle.

A pause.

He buzzed them in.

CHAPTER FIFTY-FOUR

Empty Room

Mr. Ioli walked among the remaining pods. He wanted to sit down somewhere but he didn't want to get into one. It was too creepy. He had to do something. But what?

Maybe he could ride the train somewhere, but it wasn't clear how it worked or how it even arrived. The business-like woman with the lipstick was gone after she and a few tough guys pushed the last of the pods onto a flat-bed train.

He was disappointed in how this all turned out.

He had spent years alone in his little room. He had watched it, waited for it. Strange men with strange ideas and strange needs had stolen his life. He had been selfish, afraid, alone.

He wouldn't have made his wife proud.

It hadn't always been like this. He had once worked on the docks, just before the container ships changed the city forever. He had lifted heavy bales of cotton, cold bananas, and boxes of furniture from strange places covered in strange writing. He was young then, not more than eighteen, and that's when he met his wife, a girl his age who was so pretty it looked like the sun rose in her eyes.

Her name was Rosie.

They grew older. They never had children, and they loved life. He went with her to Florida and Mexico and even as far as Paris, where he kissed her under the Eiffel Tower when they were both thirty. Years went by, she got sicker, and then the space in the bed emptied and he was alone. Then Richie the Hammer convinced him to dump those memories for security, for a sense of safety. He gave up the place he had lived in all his life for a cold room ringed with dark.

Sitting with his back against a cold steel pod, he thought about those evening walks to Sunset Park, the good smells of the apartment, the sweetness of the morning air through an open window. Then she died.

And he gave all that up. For money.

Money. He wanted to make sure he'd be safe in retirement, so he had given up polished wood and warm rugs and windows to agree with Richie the Hammer to turn his apartment into a damned hangar.

"Enough of this," he said.

Enough of what? a voice said. A girl's voice.

"Who's there?" asked Mr. Ioli.

I'm Ruth. I've been watching you. I wish I could have helped sooner.

"Where are you?"

I'm all around you. I'm with the man who died.

"Are you a ghost?"

Not quite. I'm in a coma. I heard they were keeping you here so I came to get you.

Mr. Ioli shuddered. His wife had been in a coma. "How?" he asked.

It would take too long to explain, but I can tell you I found a hole that I could use to sneak into these places. It's not important. What's important is that you're safe.

"Can I see you?"

No, that's very difficult, but I'm going to take you to people who help. A train is coming. Get on board and I'll take you where you need to go.

Mr. Ioli relaxed and walked between the pods into the dark. A train roared out of some distant tunnels and stopped in front of him, a Red Bird, one of the old subway cars. What a strange thing, to see it in tip-top shape, shining like a new penny.

All aboard, whispered the girl, the echoes bouncing through the darkness.

Mr. Ioli climbed aboard and sat down. The train rolled away from the station into the dark.

CHAPTER FIFTY-FIVE

Yes

Claude answered the door to the two teenagers and the man. He ushered them in quickly and closed the door behind them.

Claude's apartment was barely furnished. He had decided that when he moved near Industry City to build the pods that he wouldn't be staying long. He would take his money and move back to Paris ... and that's exactly what he was going to do after he spoke to these people.

"Hello," he said. "I'm the man who contacted you."

"I'm Paul. You can call me Turtle. These are my friends and this is Mr. Llorente. We were told you know something about the pods?"

"That's right. But I can't speak. I signed an agreement," said Claude.

"Those pods are being used to transport people," said Turtle. "They don't know where they're going and they don't know what will happen to them when they get there. But it's very bad. If they get into those pods they'll die. We need to stop it."

Claude nodded and then brought up the video he and the rest of the pod builders took.

"I didn't know what I was seeing but I knew it was bad. Where are those things going and why are they going?" he asked.

"That's very hard to answer," said Turtle. "You have to trust us."

Claude shut down his computer and put it into his backpack.

"Can you show us where they are?" asked Mark.

Claude paused to think for a moment. The agreement was very thorough and very scary. It required him to include a copy of his passport as well as the geographic coordinates of any other home he owned or frequented. "It's for security," he'd been told by the smiling British man who had signed them on to make the pods.

He would stay at a friend's in Paris and then figure out something later. He had enough money to buy something in Barcelona, and he had always wanted to live there. But why help these strangers, these kids? It made no sense.

Claude was an engineer though, and he only wanted to make good things. Now, as he understood it, these pods were very, very dangerous.

"I'll take you, but then I'm leaving. It's very dangerous for me to be here," said Claude. He had a ticket already in his bag.

"If you show us the pods, we can send you anywhere you want to go," said Turtle. "It'll be hard to understand, but we promise to help you."

Claude was quiet and then asked, "How?"

"It's a long story, but if you can help us, we'll tell you after everything's done. Bring what you need to travel."

"I have a plane ticket," said Claude.

"Where we're going you don't need plane tickets," said Mark, smiling. "Let's go."

Claude grabbed his backpack and led them back down the stairs onto the street again, looking both ways suspiciously. "Who are you?" he asked. "Are you with the people who hired me?"

Turtle shook his head. "No, we're not. We're trying to stop them. Those things you're making, those pods, they're vehicles. They want to send people into a place that will change them. It's very dangerous and we need to stop them."

"I knew there was something strange," said Claude.

"Very strange," said Oz as they crossed Third Avenue towards the Brooklyn warehouse district. Huge buildings loomed above them, some crisscrossed in graffiti, others carefully renovated to meld old-world design with modern touches like steel and plastic. A sign flickered in the dark - Ends Meat - and another sign pointed into a pair of double doors advertising a coffee shop called the Enola Gay. It was almost empty at this hour, but they could see groups of young people in jeans and T-shirts walking down the quiet halls.

They walked through the building into an older, more run-down part. Here the fancy offices gave way to workshops that smelled like sawdust and paint. The pod workshop was at the end of the hall, away from everyone else. Claude took out his keys and unlocked the door.

"You're sure you can get me out of here?" asked Claude ... just before the door swung open.

Mr. Goode, the man who signed the contract with him, stood there with another man, Mr. Adams, who had his hand in his coat.

"Put away the gun, Adams. We mean no harm. Claude? Where are you going?" asked Mr. Goode. "We had a contract."

"I know what you're doing," said Claude.

"What am I doing? We contracted you to build vehicles. We asked you to build them and that's all. There's nothing to fear. I'll let you go, to be certain, but I don't want you to get the wrong idea."

Claude was quiet.

Mr. Goode turned to look at the rest of the crew. Oz, Mark, Agata, and then when he saw Mr. Llorente he smiled broadly.

"Let Claude go," said Turtle. "He's useless to you."

"You're spoiling my plan again, Paul," said Mr. Goode. "It's unacceptable. And you, Mr. Llorente, so wonderful to see you."

"Get back to your hole, Goode," said Mr. Llorente. "Go back to where you hid last time. Like a rat."

"Kindness, Mr. Llorente. Kindness is what's needed now. I need you all to come with me. Claude, you'll continue to work unhindered."

"I'm done," said Claude.

"Then your team will continue to work. That's all I ask," said Mr. Goode.

As they talked, the lights seemed to flicker gently. Mark looked up and then at each of the people in the room.

We must leave here, said 411 through Mark. He had been taken again, quickly and quietly.

"What's this?" asked Mr. Goode.

Behind him, a door leaned against the wall, a double door big enough for the pods that was hammered clumsily into a wooden frame. It had been chained shut during the working day when Claude and his team were there, but now it was open and behind it was a train station with tile walls and white marble floors. Guttering gas lamps lined the back wall, and a sign said "Mytratti Portable" above the track bed, which they could not see from that angle.

Claude was mesmerized. Oz, Turtle, and Mark surrounded him while the strange voice continued.

Mr. Goode and Mr. Adams watched as the four slowly backed away from the open door. Something filled the empty space inside the door, a trick of the light at first and then something more treacherous. It was something like oil and something like fog, and it was pitch-black. It slid along the floor towards Mr. Goode and Mr. Adams, and before it could reach Oz and Turtle, they rushed Claude and Mark into the hall and slammed the workshop door shut behind them.

"Do you have a key?" asked Turtle.

Claude fumbled with the lock and latched it. There was pounding on the other side of the door and indistinct cries from within.

"What did we do?" asked Claude.

They are being taken away, not hurt, said Mark, his voice seeming to come from everywhere. *It is time for you to visit the Breach. We are close to the end.*

"Where's the Breach?" asked Turtle.

Follow me, he said, and they left the building into the gathering night.

CHAPTER FIFTY-SIX

Tunnels

Ruth had dropped off the old man and was helping another group of escapees into the Dark Station when the Mytro found her. It came in a flash, the way it had come when she first thought of it as the Demon. She didn't have time to comfort the few people who were coming out of the metal pods into the absolute dark.

How had the Demon found them? She supposed she could ask it.

Before her was the Mytro's domain, the tunnels cutting through a grey, misty place. It was like a city below her, these crisscrossing wormholes. In the distance something seethed.

Ruth smiled.

Hello, she said.

You cannot stop what will soon happen, said the Mytro. The voice was clattering tracks, the howl of brakes, a lonesome whistle.

You have no power anymore, she said. *We're about to free your slaves.*

The Mytro blazed in the distance, fire burning like a supernova.

Power? I can show you power, howled the Mytro.

She blazed. The Boy had taught her how to do it. It wasn't hard. It was a movement of energy. She could do it at will. Back in her room she was immobile. In here she was a fairy, a fire wraith. The Mytro seemed to eye her warily.

You are young. You do not understand your power, said the Mytro.

I understand that it is enough to destroy you. The Guild is in motion.

You need a host to be rid of me, said the Mytro. *What fool would sacrifice himself to take me away from here?*

Ruth had thought of that, the way it would happen. Each of the Nayzun needed a separate body, a body that could die, in order to escape. Then, that same body would have to take the Mytro away from Earth, into space, where it would be trapped forever. The process would destroy the host. She would be that body.

The Mytro curled its voice into a smile. *Now you see the problem,* it said.

There are no problems, only opportunities, she said, repeating something her father once said when she began to fall sick.

If you do not defy me, I will spare you, said the Mytro. *We can live together. We did it before, when you were young and not so headstrong.*

Things change, Ruth said. *It's time for you to go.*

She felt the Mytro shudder. She knew why it was upset, why it didn't want to go: this was its food. It had attached to Earth like a parasite and she was the vaccine, the homegrown answer created by whatever curbed power in the universe. Perhaps, one day, she would know. Until then, all she knew was that one day she became part of this strange darkness and took control of it.

How did you find the Dark Station? she asked.

I can see them, where humans go.

She thought about the oubliette, the water station where she hid the girl's father. The Mytro hadn't found that.

Realizing what she was doing, the Mytro began to pulse, a heat building up in the darkness and scalding her, somehow, even though her body was far away.

She made a new station, far off, in the dark. No humans would go there, so it was safe.

And a moment later she was gone, the Mytro raging in its way, burning, burning in the misty grey.

This is not over, it said to no one.

But it knew that the end was near. For Rosie.

CHAPTER FIFTY-SEVEN

Army

The first Nayzun, a young one, received the signal and told the others. Along the dark tunnels they moved, feet in starlight dust, their eyes glowing as they moved, glints of steel at the edges of the tunnel.

Where? Where?

They received the message through the dead air. *Forward. All the time forward.*

They came to the big place one by one, lining up and looking at each other as if for the first time. There were metal pods here, and the edges of the room were wreathed in darkness.

Was it time? Was this the moment?

Fire is coming, said one.

She is keeping us safe, said another.

There was a nod, a distant memory of once nodding. There was worry, a feeling they had not felt in years, centuries. These human movements that were so important once but were now washed away. Others remembered other motions, strange motions, water breathing through wet gills, or dust between a dozen toes. These were the newcomers, the ones the Mytro brought from distant lands to work these tunnels. They would go home as well?

A dream come true. A glad voice over a garden gate. A shrill cry echoing over rock.

They stood in the Breach, waiting.

An old man came out of the shadows. He looked at the Nayzun but was quiet. They were quiet as well.

We mean no harm, said one of the Nayzun and the old man nodded.

"Welcome to my home, what's left of it," said Mr. Ioli. The train had dropped him back at his old apartment.

The fire will not come here, said the oldest one, the first human. He wasn't even in a body, just a whisper in the wind. *Wait, my brothers and sisters, and we will be free.*

And so they waited.

Soon there were hundreds, nearly a thousand.

They stood, stalks of tall wheat in the dim lights. This was the first time they had seen each other in the light. They were so ragged, so tired. Their skin sallow, crosshatched in scars. Some were missing fingers, limbs. They had been worked so hard and for so long that they looked like the ruins of some great multi-geared machine, tumbledown and rusted.

They did not have to wait long.

CHAPTER FIFTY-EIGHT

Basement Escape

"Where do we take them?" asked Maya.

"Away from here," said Ehioze.

"Wait a second. The coordinates. Breach. That's where we need to go. That's where they can get out," said Maya. She showed Ehioze the coordinates and he put them into his phone. It was near Turtle's house.

"If Mr. Partridge researched it, then it's safe," said Ehioze. "Or at least it's important."

The men and women in the curry shop basement had formed themselves into a long line, but some of them were already heading for the upstairs door. It was a heavy metal door and locked with a bolt on the other side. Some of the people began to pound and howl, and someone fumbled with the lock on the other side.

"It's shut," said someone from the other side. "I can't move it."

A slight panic rose in the crowd.

"Please, remain calm," said Ehioze, leading four people down the stairs and back into the basement. There were about twenty people in all, and they were increasingly panicked.

"We'll be closer to Turtle, at least," said Maya.

"OK, people," Ehioze said in a louder voice. "We're going in through this door. What you are about to see will be very strange and very frightening, but I promise you will be safe. Are you ready?"

There was a murmur from the crowd.

"There's no blood, right, dear?" asked one of the women.

"No blood," said Ehioze. "It's safe."

The woman seemed satisfied.

Maya opened the door to the station and the room gasped. There were about forty people in the room, Ehioze counted, so when the train came - a Red Bird, old and well-maintained – they led twenty on board. The volunteers were stunned, gawping at the train inside a strange station that hid behind a door that was not connected to anything.

"Is this magic?" asked one man, a skinny yoga practitioner with a Mohawk.

"Something like it," said Maya.

Ehioze stayed behind to load the rest of the people, and Maya said the coordinates out loud. In a moment the train rolled into the dark and they were there, among the shining pods in the Brooklyn Breach. As they left the train, there were howls of fear from the twenty volunteers on board.

Surrounding the pods, lit by dim overhead lights, was a horde of tall, grey figures, their eyes glowing with white rushlight, their mouths and ears covered in pearlescent skin. And there, standing amid this group of strange, stalk-like creatures, was a little old man.

"Well, it's about time you got here," said the old man, smiling. "This is just about the best thing I've ever seen in my life. I'm Bernie."

CHAPTER FIFTY-NINE

Promises

As the workshop filled up with darkness, Mr. Goode and Adams worked to get out. The darkness flowed out of the station like oil, glinting chitinously in the overheads.

"What do we do?" yelled Mr. Adams. He had seen this stuff before and it was never good.

"We've got to break through," said Mr. Goode, pulling out a small gun and aiming at the lock. He was about to pull the trigger when a wave of heat blew over them both, singeing them and sending them sprawling to the floor. The blackness was gone.

Finish what you promised, said the Mytro. It spoke in the fire.

"We will," said Mr. Goode. His voice wavering.

Time grows short. The Other is growing in power. You will not be forgiven for failure.

The fire burnt away the blackness, turning it to ash but catching parts of the workshop on fire. A stack of wood began to smolder, smoke, and burn. Computers along the walls began to melt, and the steel press, a gargantuan machine in the corner, hissed and gave up its internal pressure, sending the egg-shaped mold crashing down onto the floor.

"Through the door!" yelled Mr. Goode.

"And be burnt?" asked Mr. Adams.

"It's safer than sitting still!" he yelled, and they ran through the fire into the station, both of them red with the flame, their hair and clothes smoking. Mr. Goode slammed the station doors shut and a train roared up.

Finish what you promised, said the Mytro as they boarded and headed to the Breach.

CHAPTER SIXTY

Express

Turtle, Oz, Mark, and Claude headed to another station called "Ship-yards" near the workshops that was hidden in an alley between two massive buildings. A moment later they were at the Brooklyn Breach, the address given to them by 411.

It is time to finish this, said 411 through Mark.

They disembarked and saw the riot of men, women, and Nayzun. Agata and Mr. Llorente were there, and as the train left, another train brought Ehioze and Maya along with twenty additional pale Brits. It was a full house. People milled about, some screaming, some touching the Nayzun as they wandered among the stalk-like bodies. One woman was crying and praying with a bright smile on her tear-streaked face.

Then, as if a light switch had been thrown, a voice echoed through the room, a girl's voice.

She was laughing.

Hello, everyone. Welcome to Brooklyn! I need you all to move away from the train tracks and please don't touch the Nayzun. They're a bit skittish. Things are going to get a little weird here and I don't want anyone to be hurt.

Her voice came up around them like cool water. Turtle smiled, despite himself.

What's going to happen is fairly simple. These kind souls, these Nayzun, will be leaving us. They're going to move through my body and into a different place.

It will be quite alarming at first, but understand I'm freeing them. If anything bad happens, if there are flames or fires or anything, I'll take care of you. Please understand that this is a fairly unique situation you're seeing. Please don't worry. I'm here to protect you. Can I get a cheer if you understand?

The group of men and women cheered, softly, their voices echoing in the Breach. The Nayzun swayed in space, expectant.

"Hey," yelled Mr. Ioli. "I don't get it."

Turtle turned to him. "I'm Paul. I live in Brooklyn. What's about to happen is we're going to destroy a world-eating transportation system with some weird power nobody understands. It's going to get crazy."

"I'm Bernard Ioli. Bernie. I lived here. What's going to happen here? What does she mean her body?" he asked.

"There are two ways to think about this place, Mr. Ioli," said Agata's father. "I've been studying this for years and have found that what we see here, all of this all around us, is actually an illusion. It's a way for our minds to process this thing, whatever you want to call it, but it is really a series of wormholes, all connected, that are controlled by a central force.

"So it's like the New York Subway controlled by the Transit Authority," said Mr. Ioli. He had a thick Brooklyn accent and he coughed a little. He hadn't used his voice in a while.

"Exactly, except not exactly," said Mr. Llorente. "These stations don't exist. When we enter them, our brains create an approximation of the station that they expect to see. But in reality, we aren't taking up any space at all. That's why, for example, they could fit that entire hangar into your apartment. You were existing inside the equivalent of a dent in the space-time continuum. It was made very big by certain people for a certain purpose."

"So what are we doing?"

Mr. Llorente looked around.

"Well, for one, we're going to destroy this room."

"What about my old place?"

"I suppose this was once your apartment. That's all gone now."

"And what do you need to do?"

"Nothing, as far as I can tell," said Mr. Llorente. "The voice you heard, that is the voice of someone who is taking care of everything that is happening here. I think we trust her."

"Sounds pretty silly. I haven't trusted a single person since all of this started," said Mr. Ioli. "Are you all safe?"

"We're going to be fine," said Turtle.

And with those words, Mr. Goode, Mr. Adams, and Mr. Watson rolled into the Breach, guns drawn. Following them was a ball of fire so huge it burned the very air around them all. The people and the Nayzun screamed.

"All right friends," yelled Mr. Goode. "Play time's over."

CHAPTER SIXTY-ONE

Pop

Mr. Goode and Mr. Adams stepped out of the train. He looked around, eyed the Nayzun and the humans as the flames seemed to curl around him, surrounding him but not touching him. He was mad-eyed, ready to fight. Mr. Adams' gun bobbed softly, uncertain. More fire roared out of the tunnel.

The train roared away. It was burning.

Somewhere, a wind moved. Another train approached and a team of men twenty in black poured off. They had guns and they aimed them at the Nayzun.

"This place is about to be closed down. I'd suggest we all leave calmly," said Mr. Goode.

"Goode," said Mr. Llorente. "Stop this! You can't do this."

"I can and will, Ernesto. Thank you for coming back to help," he said.

The Nayzun, unmoving, seemed unperturbed.

"You're not going to do this," said Turtle.

Mr. Goode lifted his arms. "I am and it's happening. Anyone who wants to survive must leave immediately. Except for the volunteers."

He stood like a strange god in the fire. The volunteers from the restaurant shrieked and one ran to the front door, Mr. Ioli's old door, and tried to leave. It was locked.

Then, in a moment, the bubble in which Mr. Goode stood popped. The flames closed in on Mr. Goode and his men and then raged higher.

Enough, said Ruth. *This ends now.*

And in a moment, everything changed.

CHAPTER SIXTY-TWO

Standoff

Turtle looked down. He, Agata, Ehioze, Oz, Maya, Mr. Ioli, and Mr. Llorente were standing on a beam of light in the middle of darkness. Claude was a few yards away, backpack still in hand. It was dizzying to be in this position, suspended above nothing, looking down at nothing. Their bodies seemed to glow green in the crepuscular light. But they could not be afraid.

Turtle exhaled and so did Agata. Ehioze whistled, quietly. Oz cursed, muttering something under his breath.

A girl stood before them. Next to them stood Mr. Partridge.

They could see through him.

Hello, Ernesto, he said, smiling.

"Hello, old friend. Does it hurt?" asked Mr. Llorente.

Not in the least. It's actually quite amusing.

"You were always good at making the best of things," said Mr. Llorente.

Stiff upper lip, etcetera, said Mr. Partridge.

A moment later and the scene changed. They were in a different place and there were more people and Nayzun here.

Below them was the Gusano, the Worm Hole, the place where humans first discovered the Mytro. It was an earthen hold, tiny, far away. They stood above it and Turtle felt that he could step out into the dark and fall directly down into it. Next to them were the Nayzun, now in the hundreds, and the forty men and women. Everyone was screaming but no one could make a sound.

This is the place where it hides, said Ruth. *The Nayzun have to take a body to transfer away from here. They will use mine.*

"But that will kill you," said Mr. Llorente.

Perhaps, but it's a choice I'm willing to make. Once I'm done I'll need you to take these men and women home.

"What's happening?" asked Mr. Ioli.

"We need to free these creatures. They need a human host to cling to before they leave their Nayzun bodies and the process is very dangerous. Rose is risking her life for these creatures."

"Then let me do it," said Mr. Ioli. "I spent most of my life doing nothing. I want to finally do something."

Winds picked up around them and some of the Nayzun struggled and fell.

We don't have much time. The Mytro is coming. I'll do it.

"Don't you dare," said Mr. Ioli. "I'll do what needs to be done," he said. His voice was barely audible, as if they were in a vacuum.

So you have finally made it, said the Mytro. It was a voice like a thunderclap, and they heard it their heads, not through their ears. *You have come to my dominion.*

Turtle remembered what had worked before. He opened his mouth and began to sing the old songs that made the Mytro, that charmed it. Ehioze and Agata joined in.

The Mytro laughed, coldly. *You're trying those old tricks? I've hardened myself against your silly songs. You don't even know what you are singing. Those are the old words, the words that formed me and my brothers. I chose this place, you know. I chose this place to help your puny race grow. I built the first networks here and waited. I waited and waited. When I grew impatient, I came out and saw that you were little better than apes – brainless, mindless. I showed myself, and you cowered. When I came here, I was an angel. Fire and smoke were my helpmates, demons in my thrall. A few centuries here and I've been reduced to nothing. You humans take everything and burn it out, destroy it. You do not deserve this.*

I had heard of this, long ago. One of my brothers on another planet had been destroyed in the same way, cut down in his prime by an illness borne of men.

And so you are the illness, said the Mytro. *I will cleanse you. Do you not fear my fire?*

We don't, said Ruth. *I'm holding you back.*

Somewhere in the dark a fire blazed and was put out.

But you have no conduit. Your mission is failed, said the Mytro.

"I'm the one," said Mr. Ioli, stepping forward as the air grew thicker. They could hear sound again.

"We know your secrets," said Agata to an empty sky. "We can send you away. We don't want you."

If you unmake me here, I will go elsewhere, said the Mytro. For the first time Turtle noticed that the voice was a woman's, calm and cool under the deep boom as each word rolled through their minds. The train noises were gone.

"I don't need to unmake you. I know what you are. You were the ghost in the cave, under the Hill of Winds. We can return you there. No forward, no back, no Nayzun, no helpers. Trapped, just as you were at the dawn of time," said Mr. Llorente.

You don't have that power. And why? I am the Queen of the Ways, the Giver of Motion. I'm not your enemy, said the Mytro. It was calm and steady, without emotion. *Our kind are older than your planet. We were tasked with carrying information from star to star, galactic connectors who, in turn, sent the message back up to the highest ones. But the highest ones have been silent for eons. So we build and destroy, build and destroy, again and again. If you and your friends aim to kill me, you'd best bring your best weapons to the fray because I will not forgive failure.*

"You are a curse," said Mr. Llorente.

Fine. Destroy me. And then what? The Mytro crumbles. The rails disappear. You humans, who love this plaything so, will be stuck getting around on your own primitive power. The Builder is a girl. She has no dominion here.

"That's a price we'll pay," said Agata. "After all, girls can do anything."

Try and I will burn you.

Oz gulped.

"Take a deep breath, Oz," said Turtle. "It'll be fine."

"Am I doing what I think I'm doing," asked Mr. Ioli.

Yes, if you can, said Ruth. *I need to hold it off.*

"And everyone will be safe?" asked Mr. Ioli.

Yes, said Ruth.

"Who has my dog?" he asked.

"We do," said Turtle.

"Take care of her," said Mr. Ioli.

Thank you, Bernie.

"Don't mention it," he said.

Mr. Partridge smiled.

I'll help you, Bernie, he said. *I don't think I want to stay here much longer. Just follow me and we'll get it done.*

Mr. Partridge seemed to merge with Mr. Ioli in the dark. The ghost rode Mr. Ioli like 411 rode Mark and together they walked towards the Nayzun who now moved towards the old man. Their arms reached out toward him and Turtle could hear them whispering to themselves.

Thank you, they said.

Mr. Ioli understood with clarity his purpose. As the humans watched, the Nayzun dissolved and Mr. Ioli seemed to change. His body was stiff then loose. He fell to the ground, his face changing. He smiled and then frowned, his brow wrinkling and growing slack. And as the Nayzun moved through him, they died, one by one, and the whispering of praise and thanks seemed to roar in the air.

And the Mytro crackled and hummed and then, finally, disappeared.

Somewhere at the blazing heart of a strange light, Mr. Ioli opened a wooden door and walked through into an apartment done up just so, polished to a golden shine, full of good things forever, a meal cooked by a pretty girl that he loved with all the drops of water in the ocean. And the drops quenched the fire and it was quiet.

He was home.

CHAPTER SIXTY-THREE

It's All around Me

Mr. Ioli was gone. Somewhere in the tunnels the Mytro screamed and was silenced. It seemed to quick, so sudden.

They were alone.

"Is that it?" asked Oz.

"I think so?" said Turtle.

They above the Gusano, the Worm Hole, and listened for any sign of fire or howling or fear. It did not come.

"What happened?" asked Maya.

"A sacrifice," said Mark. "A sacrifice."

A train rolled into along the light and stopped in front of them. It was suspended in the dark in front of them, like a magic trick.

"Are we going?" asked Agata.

Mr. Llorente nodded.

"The Nayzun were trapped," he said. "They needed to connect to a free body to escape. And so Mr. Ioli sacrificed himself. Without Nayzun, the Mytro can't exist. The Nayzun are the Mytro's eyes, ears, and hands. Goode thought he could make his own Nayzun and make the Mytro beholden to him. He thought he could cut a deal with the devil but it failed."

"And Mr. Partridge? 411?" asked Turtle.

Mark looked around.

"Gone, both gone," he said. "I'd be able to tell. I don't sense Rose, either."

The forty men and women boarded the train and another dozen appeared from out of nowhere, winked into existence. They were naked and hustled into another train. Turtle's face went red.

"Who are those people?" he asked.

No one answered.

"This is weird as heck," said Oz.

The boarded and the train dinged, its doors hissing closed. As the train began to roll, laughter filled the cabin and began to shake the windows – wild laughter, mad with anger and defeat.

CHAPTER SIXTY-FOUR

What's Left

Fire surrounded the train. People screamed. Claude looked out the window and howled.

"We're going to die!" someone cried, but they did not die.

The train disappeared from around them and they were left suspended in a vast matrix of lines. These were the Mytro lines stripped of their reality, just lines of light that went from place to place. It was all that was left of the Mytro. At the vertices were the Mytro stations and they could see each one in miniature, as if they were looking at a dollhouse full of thousands of rooms.

The fire went out in an instant, seeming to curl on itself like a red fern, the leaves of smoke rolling back in on themselves and retreating into the dark.

Stop it, yelled the girl, Rose. *You've lost.*

I will not. This is mine. All of this. I made it, howled the Mytro.

Then I will unmake it, said Rose.

Mr. Llorente cried out to stop her but she ignored him. His voice was torn away by the noise she made as she showed herself in the tunnels.

She was gigantic now, a girl looming over the green skeins of track that were suspended in space. She wore a white robe and her hair floated around her head as if she were suspended in water. She looked at the thousands of stations arrayed at the vertices and pointed to them, one at a time, winking them out.

With each wave of her hand another part of the Mytro disappeared.

"We'll die," said Oz. "She's destroying the stations."

"We're not in a station," sait Turtle. "We're above it all. We can't disappear if we're not in a station."

Stop this! I forbid it, howled the Mytro.

You are in no position to forbid anything, monster. Leave here.

I was here first, said the Mytro. It was almost petulant, thought Turtle.

"Turtle, Agata, your keys. Help her," said Mr. Llorente.

"How?" asked Agata. She pulled her key, an ornate clockwork thing, and held it in her hand. It was vibrating now, as if it were an alarm clock ringing.

"You'll amplify her power. That's what they're for," said Mr. Llorente.

The two aimed their keys at various stations, near and far, and they winked out. The Brooklyn Breach disappeared, taking Mr. Goode and his men with it. The stops along Central Park, in the heart of Paris, everywhere.

One after the other they disappeared. Until Rose turned her attention to the Gusano.

The Mytro screamed. For a moment it appeared before then, a gigantic woman, her face wreathed in fire, old and jagged as a rock face, as veined in fire and lightning.

Rose pointed to the Gusano.

The Mytro shrank to the size of a mouse and disappeared on the dirt floor of the Gusano.

Turtle and Agata aimed their keys at the Gusano and the felt a surge of energy that flowed through them and into Rose.

The Gusano, the place where the network took root, disappeared. The Mytro went with it.

Rose exhaled, growing smaller and smaller. She now stood before them, a girl, translucent, her face drawn and white.

"Are you OK?" asked Oz.

"Is it over?" asked Maya.

It's over, said Rose. *I sent it away. Mr. Goode is gone, too. The Brooklyn Breach is closed.*

"Thank you, Rose," said Mr. Llorente.

"How will we get home?" asked Mark.

The rails are still here, but the ghost in them is gone and the stations are gone. I can make a few stations for you. And then replace the broken ones. Wait a second. I have some people who want to thank you.

From out of the darkness they felt the rustling of countless ghosts. They heard thousands of voices in countless languages. Many of them thanked them, whispering their appreciation into the warm, close air. Others sent images - smiling babies, a strange six-legged horse with the head of a dog, a verdant jungle full of miasmic creatures made entirely of plasma.

"Those are all the Nayzun," said Agata. "They're free."

Mr. Llorente nodded. He waved at the dark and it seemed to wave back, to cheer, to thank them again and again for freedom.

CHAPTER SIXTY-FIVE

Juttering

A train came. None of them were expecting it. It came out of the dark and rode one of the lights that now made up the Mytro. It was missing a wheel and clattered in like something out of a junkyard, stopping slowly, the brakes smoking and the metal howling as if it would tear itself apart.

It would be hard to understand the Mytro, now. Rose was the one who was building it. It was a new thing, completely different.

Turtle read somewhere that the brain was a physical structure. Doctors could shut it down, freeze it, and then, a few hours later, wake up the patient, who would be fine. The brain was a physical thing, one built up by years of living. All it needed was the electricity, the life force running through it, to start back up. That was the Mytro - a brain controlled by a life force. The original force was gone, but now the Builder was on the scene and she could fix things, make them better. At least that's how Turtle understood it.

Mark wasn't so sure. "Is this safe?" he asked.

"It is. It's going to take a few months to get things back to normal. Now that the original Mytro is gone, things aren't going to be the same," said Turtle.

"Who will fix the stations? Who will fix the trains?" asked Mark.

"I think that will solve itself," Turtle told him. "The Builder said that it didn't even need Nayzun, that the Nayzun weren't actually part of the original plan. Something dark made the Nayzun, darker and more powerful than the original Mytro."

They clattered into the dark, the train loping and juttering. Turtle was the first to request a ride home. He said the name of his station, and a moment later they were there. It was a stop that the Builder made on the fly. She called it Turtle's House. This was the stop where he had first boarded the Mytro with Mr. Kincaid, those many months ago.

"You two were very brave, and I appreciate all you've done, Turtle," said Mr. Llorente. "It wasn't easy, I know."

"It wasn't, but it was worth it. I'm glad you're all together."

Mark looked around. "Where are we?"

"Bay Ridge Avenue and Fifth," said Turtle. "I could get you closer to the station but there are no stations anymore. We have to build new ones."

"I think I'll just walk," said the monk. "Just get me out of here. I've had enough train travel for one day. But the Guild will be in touch?"

"I'll make sure of it," said Mr. Llorente.

"I'd like to help out if I can, in the future," said Mark.

Turtle nodded. They were quiet for a moment, then Turtle hugged Agata for a long time. She kissed him on the cheek first and then she kissed Oz.

"I'll see you in Barcelona," she said.

"Maybe you can come hang out here a bit too?" Oz said.

Agata blushed.

Mark and Turtle got off the train and walked out of the station into the alley. It was dark, late in the evening. They stood there for a moment, taking a breath.

"Thank you for all you've shown me, Turtle," said Mark as he shook the boy's hand.

"It was fun, right?"

"What I remember of it, absolutely," said Mark.

Mark began walking north, towards his temple. Turtle started walking home. It took a minute to walk down the dark avenue and his phone beeped. His grandmother had left a voicemail, so he listened to it. She said she had left the back door open.

He walked down the long, quiet driveway to the back of the house. A cat was rustling somewhere in the bushes by the other side of the house, and Turtle remembered another stand of bushes that had led him to his first visit to the Mytro. He shook his head. Things had changed. He'd have to deal with the Kincaids again at school, but maybe this time they'd believe him.

He opened the door as quietly as he could, stopping it just before he knew it would squeak. He knew every step of this old house, every broken board and every telltale step. He walked quietly across the kitchen and up the living room steps. The hallway was dark, and he heard his grandmother stir.

"Paul? Is that you?" she said, sleep in her voice.

"I'm home. Sorry. I got caught up."

"OK, if you're hungry, there's food," she said. He could hear her getting out of bed, and he walked up to her door and peeked in.

"Don't get up. I'm fine. I'm not very hungry."

"You're going to have to tell me what you get up to this late one of these days, Paul," she said.

"Research," said Turtle.

"Research my foot. We'll talk in the morning."

His face flushed. Maybe it was time to tell her. He decided he would once the Builder had cleaned things up a little. He didn't want to scare her.

He walked down the hall to his room and took off his clothes, which needed to be washed. They were covered in mud.

He thought of Agata and her father, how happy they would be coming back together again. He thought of his own parents, gone so many years now as to be truly lost in time's oubliette. But he had a family. He had his grandmother. His friends. His best friend.

And he was alive and well and very, very sleepy. His head hit the pillow and he slept. If he dreamed, he didn't remember it. When he opened his eyes, hungry and thirsty, his grandmother standing over him.

"You look like you fell into a mud puddle," she said, holding up his jeans.

"I slipped," he said, lifting himself up on an elbow. It was 2:00 a.m., and the sun was about to flash through his window onto the bedcovers.

She looked down at him through her glasses. "Is everything OK?" she asked.

Turtle nodded, although he knew it was a lie. "I just had a long day, I guess," he said.

"Well, if you need to talk about it, I'm here," she said. "Your mother used to come in and we'd talk for hours. I'd like it if we did that every few weeks. Just so I can keep up with you. It seems like you're all over the place with your friends and your school and I hardly know where you are anymore."

"I guess that's true. Maybe once school is out I'll be a little less stressed."

"Knowing you the way I know you, I doubt that very much. But it will be a lot nicer for you to be at home where I can keep my eye on you. It's dangerous out there for teenagers, and you're my little teenager."

"Not yet, Grandma."

"Close enough," she said. She kissed him on the forehead and went down the creaking stairs to the kitchen.

CHAPTER SIXTY-SIX

Sleep, Perchance to Dream

A week later a full moon rose over the big house in Leinster Terrace. Ms. Banister looked out the window for a moment. The cool of winter was now approaching, but it was nice to keep the windows open a crack some nights when it wasn't too cold, drafts be damned. She took a deep breath and then turned back to her charge.

The Builder was asleep in a beautifully appointed bed, partly clinical and partly luxurious. Her hair had been cut and washed, and she now wore soft robes that would stop the bedsores. A nurse, a Friend of the Mytro who had lived alone for years, volunteered to organize twenty-four-hour supervision, and the Guild bought the Builder all the equipment she needed to stay alive. It was a carefully wrought sick room for a very important patient.

Perhaps soon they would tell the world about this amazing girl and her amazing power. Until then she would be ceaselessly comfortable. The Guild owed her that.

The day nurse had arranged a spray of flowers on a small table, and they rouged the air with the scent of jasmine and orchids. It was a rare, cloudless night in London, and the city could not drown out every star. There were a few in the corners of the window, peeking past the orange murk of the city lights.

It hadn't taken long to get the Builder situated in her new home. When Ms. Banister had proposed moving the Builder, her father had immediately jumped at the chance to get his daughter into a "top-notch facility," his own words. The Guild had told him that they were a nonprofit group that attempted to help the neediest and that they would care for the girl and send him money every month to help with his own expenses. It was an amazing offer, one that a less addled and exhausted caretaker might have looked at in puzzlement. But luckily the Guild all had kind voices, and they kept their promises. The Builder was in a beautiful room and would be well cared for, and the father, when he saw where his daughter was and that she was safe, was very happy. He promised to come monthly - the Guild would even buy his plane tickets - but they doubted he would take them up on the offer.

That night, after all the help had gone to bed, the Builder spoke to Ms. Banister.

The Builder stirred in her sleep, and Ms. Banister came to her, gliding over the hard, wooden floor in her delicate ballet flats. She reached out and touched the Builder's hand and then brushed a strand of hair away from her face.

Ms. Banister thought of Mr. Partridge, now gone. How he would have loved the thought that the Guild were taking care of their own Mytratta, this beautiful woman who, for a decade, had been trapped in her own body and was now joyfully free.

The moonlight came through the window and a beam rested on her duvet. The Builder stirred, and her eyelids fluttered open for a moment. She couldn't see anything - she stared straight ahead - but Ms. Banister knew she was there. She could feel a warm presence somewhere nearby, the feeling you get when you've entered a room that a loved one has just left or the way you can tell someone is watching television downstairs - the muffled voices, the flash of music, and, most important, the buzzing electricity of something purring in the dark.

Ms. Banister touched the Builder's hand and her eyes closed. She stirred again, and the machines that kept her alive hissed for a moment, lay silent, and then hissed again. Again and again, breath coming in and out in the dark, moonlit room.

The Builder dreamed. Inside herself, she was in a little room with a wooden floor. There was a little table and a cabinet of curiosities. There was an old arrowhead that she had once seen, long ago. There was a little doll made of ceramic and dressed in blue. There was a photograph of the children she had met, Turtle and Agata. They were holding hands. She had a China tea set and a tablecloth and a little pot of tea. She was content, and she was happy.

And so, the green skein of the Mytro grew and grew and grew and the tunnels were silent, empty except for the rushing trains roaring from station to station in the dark.

Epilogue

The man in brown shorts and a tan shirt walked alone under a cloudless red sky. His face was covered by a black breather, and he wore big goggles now dusted with fine powder. The air here was oxygen-rich but thick with dust, so he had to wear something to keep from coughing. Why this place had no flora or fauna wasn't clear. Perhaps the water was buried. Or perhaps the life here existed in some other form.

He carried a tan backpack and had a metal rod in his hand that he was using to test the azure earth in front of him. There were pockets here and there that would collapse into little wormholes that bored through the crust of this empty planet, and he worried that if he stepped in one he would hurt himself - twist an ankle or break a foot and then he would be stuck forever.

Finding Mytro stops on this planet was difficult. They were inside natural tunnels created by the flow of old water and lava. The first he found by dumb luck. He had nearly stumbled into a deep, wide hole that opened in front of him, and he slid down it into an open space. He sketched the station before he went farther and tried to take a photograph on his cell phone. He was trying to keep the battery from running down - here on this planet, electronics seemed to discharge faster than anywhere else - so he turned it on briefly, took a few shots, and then turned it off, tucking it back into a soft plastic pouch he had purchased on Earth at a camping shop.

When he first began exploring, he would find himself in strange, empty places. It took him days to dampen the fears he felt as he trudged.

It was in the tunnels that he found water.

This planet had no Nayzun that he could see. The stations were quiet except for the burble of invisible water and the occasional whoosh of air through the darkness. The stations themselves looked like glass bubbles. The trains were long tubes of sapphire and emerald, strangely cold, and when they arrived in the station, a scrim of frost formed on them for an instant and then quickly faded in the warmer air. There were no seats, only odd handholds along the lower part of the train wall. There were no tracks, just a small stream of water flowing into the darkness on either side of the platform. The trains were silent, a far cry from the screaming clatter of the Mytro on Earth.

He had found three stations, just by imagining features on the planet he had seen after wandering in a wide circle around other Mytro stops. *Take me to the blue spire to the north*, he'd say, and the Mytro would comply as closely as it could, dropping him in another odd station where he could get out and look around and then record the location on a map he was making of the terrain. This planet had an odd magnetic field, so north wasn't quite north, but he made do, noting the deviations in his log book.

But now he walked outside, in the open air. He loved to walk here. It was so quiet, so strange. He was the only living thing he could see on the otherwise smooth desert of blue dust pocked by the holes that popped open and set out a burst of cold air.

He prepared to camp for the night. He had a tent and a sleeping bag, and he did not need his sleeping pad. This dust was soft and sifting, and it was often more comfortable to simply lie inside the bag. The nights were warm on this planet, the days quite comfortable. Once, on waking up, he thought he saw a figure on a far-off ridge, but after he blinked the sleep from his eyes, the figure disappeared. He made a note to visit that ridge later in the week.

Now, though, he stopped and looked at the sky. There would be a few more hours of light left. It was time to take down his thoughts. He had a lot to tell the world back home.

The man pulled a notebook from his book bag. On its cover were the words "Kincaid Urban Archeology." Glued to the front cover was a photograph printed on glossy paper of a boy and a girl looking into the lens with a wary trepidation. He had written "For Them" under their faces. On the page below, he had written two words: "Never again."

He was exploring for them, and for his nephews, and for the future. He was using the Mytro for its intended use: to help propel the poor dumb animals called humans into the stars. And he understood enough to know that he nor anyone else could control it. They could harness it, however, and use it ... until it turned on them.

He pulled out a pen, wet its tip with his tongue, and began to write, the scratching of metal on paper for now the only sound drifting in the cool wind, his lines punctuated by the popping of far-off wormholes.

Made in the USA
Middletown, DE
16 February 2019